To

My dear friend
Eric B.

Best wishes

JOURNEY HOME

Dev

JOURNEY HOME

Dev Delay

AuthorHouse™
1663 Liberty Drive
Bloomington, IN 47403
www.authorhouse.com
Phone: 1-800-839-8640

© 2011 by Dev Delay. All rights reserved.

No part of this book may be reproduced, stored in a retrieval system, or transmitted by any means without the written permission of the author.

First published by AuthorHouse   08/19/2011

ISBN: 978-1-4567-8860-5 (sc)
ISBN: 978-1-4567-8861-2 (ebk)

Printed in the United States of America

Any people depicted in stock imagery provided by Thinkstock are models, and such images are being used for illustrative purposes only.
Certain stock imagery © Thinkstock.

This book is printed on acid-free paper.

Because of the dynamic nature of the Internet, any web addresses or links contained in this book may have changed since publication and may no longer be valid. The views expressed in this work are solely those of the author and do not necessarily reflect the views of the publisher, and the publisher hereby disclaims any responsibility for them.

For the young people I had the privilege of working with and the young people I hope to work with again in the future

ACKNOWLEDGMENTS

I relied on the knowledge and experience of the many British South Asian young people while writing this book, and thank them for their contributions. I'm not able to name each and everyone. Eric Blakeley, my friend and guide, always at hand to read the manuscript, and suggest ideas for improvements. Deirdre Nuttall for the editing.

My family for putting up with me for spending so much time on the computer. My relatives in India and the UK for their encouragement. My beautiful grandchildren for making me rich with happiness. I would like to pay a special tribute to my sponsor, Peter Sandhu to whom I'm indebited.

where I played hide and seek with my friends.

JOURNEY HOME

Home

It's been almost half a century since I left my mother country, my birthplace. I have been planning for years to make this journey; waiting, dreaming, scheming. Somehow, other things always got in the way.

Finally I am here, in the land of my forefathers, the land where I played with my friends hide-and-seek amongst the mango trees, the place where I rose to the burning morning sun every day.

Peacocks danced under the rainbow sky,
I ran around and got drenched in the monsoon rain.
At last, I am home and it feels good.
I arrive at my home, excited, with a spring in my step. I take large strides with a smile on my face from ear to ear, looking to pick up where I left off all those years ago.
There is no stopping me now.
My people, I shake their hands.
I hug them all, one by one.
I head for the old house through rows of sugar cane and I pass the graveyard.
On the way I see a group of children playing cricket.
I stop to talk with them.
They gaze blankly at me, and then one of them asks, unscripted, innocent, if I'm lost.

ix

Dev Delay

They let me bat and, to my embarrassment, I am out for a duck. They cheer and laugh at me. An Anglo-Indian clown in my own back yard.

It is nothing like I remember.
Nobody recognizes me.
I am invisible in my own village.
Nothing is the same, I have lost my past.
Everything has changed, been rearranged.
The mango trees are not to be seen.

The village pond has been replaced by a large house.
They say the owner moved to live in America.
The front gates are locked with padlocks.

There are many brand new stately houses in the village.
All empty and locked up, out of reach of the locals. The owners all live overseas, in the West.
I can't locate my childhood friends.
No one knows where they have gone; it's not what I expected.
Someone or something has put a spell on my past. I am so disappointed, I am lost.
All my dreams are shattered; I've become an emperor of nowhere.
I have sinned, I am being punished.
I run to the temple, as sure as fate I will pray myself out of this mess, horror. I ask forgiveness. I make a large donation to the temple's funds for the development of rest rooms for journey-makers like myself.
I reach my old house; nothing remains, only the crumbling walls covered with weeds. A black crow takes wing from a nimm tree and startles me for a second.

I take a deep breath and begin sifting through the rubble, hoping to find something belonging to me from the old days.

Nothing, nothing at all, only the memories of yesterday.

Finally, I head for the bus stop, my thoughts reflecting on days gone by. I pass a beggar, sick in the street, holding out his hand for help or forgiveness; he is my own reflection.

CHAPTER ONE

It was early March and bitterly cold. London's Heathrow Airport was packed with passengers in queues for checking in, with others standing around, waiting to see off their loved ones. Outside, heavy snow had been falling continuously for the past twenty-four hours. The snow weighed heavily on the airport buildings and the snow ploughs had been busy trying to clear the runways. Many flights had had to be cancelled. Naj arrived early and was keeping his eye on the overhead information monitors for the news about his BA flight. The monitors were telling passengers to wait for further information. He was apprehensive, his head ached, and he was not sure about what was going to happen, but tried to remain positive about the flight. After a three hour delay, Naj checked in his baggage and, with his boarding card, headed to the restaurant on the second floor. There he ordered himself a full English breakfast with coffee, minus bacon. His belly was full, his spirits were high; he was ready for the journey ahead.

*

The plane was taking Naj towards the Motherland he knew nothing about other than what he had heard in his parents conversations: A strange land with all sorts of ancient customs and traditions. A land that wasn't his. He didn't speak the language and didn't belong there. He had seen many images on TV of poor people and how they lived. Now he was on his way there to see and experience everything for himself.

After a nine hour flight, the plane landed at Delhi airport. Naj was excited as he walked into the airport behind the other passengers. After collecting his luggage he joined the long immigration queue. Inside the airport there were people everywhere. Naj couldn't believe his eyes. Thousands of people under one roof! It was a culture shock. *Where have they all come from?* He wondered. *They can't all be visiting or on holiday at the same time as me.* It was not conceivable that there were so many human beings in one space. It reminded him of an ants' nest in his back garden on a hot day, with thousands of ants running around. The airport was crowded in the extreme. It was like Oxford Street in London on the first day of the New Year sales. It was madness, madness and more madness; people were rushing around, ducking, diving, pushing and shoving each other. It was strange that no one took any notice. No one seemed to care, it was everyone for themselves. On top of it all, the heat was unbearable. He had been told about the heat before leaving the UK, but Indian heat is not like the heat of June in England. It's hotter than the hottest vindaloo. It's like being in a sauna.

Oh shit, Naj thought. *It's a bloody nightmare. How the fuck am I going to get through three weeks in this shit hole? Why, oh why did I let my parents talk me into this? I don't like this. I don't like it at all. I feel sick.* Would he be able to handle it? He was dressed in jeans and a T-shirt, but that didn't stop the sweat rolling down his back. He felt like stripping off, then looked around and decided against it. He was not prepared for the heat or the human congestion.

Journey Home

The immigration queue moved at a snail's pace, frustrating him and everyone else. After an hour it was his turn to be interrogated Indian-style. A style with a chili flavor and an attitude guaranteed to get anyone's back up. He couldn't breathe with the heat and the sweat continued to pour off his body. His t-shirt and underwear were soaked in sweat, making him feel very uncomfortable. He was out of his comfort zone. He had had no concept of India before getting on the plane. After an hour and half, he was already pissed off with India. He found himself asking the same questions over and over again: "What the fuck am I doing here in a strange land, in the heat? I should be in bed with my Lucy, a crateful of beer at my side. This has to be a dream. A dream or a nightmare."

Naj finally reached the immigration officer who gave him a cold glare and said, "Where have you come from, sir?"

"England."

"How much money have you brought with you?"

By now Naj was really pissed off with the line of questioning. He was disgusted. He could not understand why the officer was asking him about money. Wasn't that irrelevant? He wanted to give him a piece of his mind, but decided to be diplomatic. He politely asked the officer to stamp his passport so he could escape the heat inside the airport. The officer gave him another cold glare, reluctantly stamped his passport and rudely threw it back at him. Anger simmered and Naj wanted to tell him what he really thought about his behavior, but wisely chose to bite his tongue. He collected his documents and baggage and headed for the exit doors. *Fucking tosser* he thought to himself, pushing through the swing doors and into the fresher air.

Outside, more chaos greeted him and the cooler air he had been waiting for turned out to be hot, heavy and polluted. He couldn't breathe. He almost exploded with anger. The thought of returning straight to England entered his mind there and then. As soon as he stepped outside he was surrounded by four or five men of various sizes, all dressed in similar clothing. Amongst them was one with an enormous turban who wore his handlebar moustache as if it had the mystical power of protecting him from his enemies like a Maharaja. The turbaned man tried to manhandle Naj by grabbing his baggage. Naj's grip tightened; he was nervous and scared and almost panicked. "Get your greasy hands off my things, you asshole!" he shouted at the man as he squared up to him. The man gave him a hard stare. Naj couldn't make out what was happening. He was being robbed in broad daylight in front of thousands of people and no one was taking any notice! Even the security guards couldn't be bothered and just stood there doing sod all. These muggers were offering him a hotel to stay at and a taxi service to get him there, all at reasonable British rates. They fought amongst themselves for the rights to his custom. He told them he didn't need any of their services and that all he was looking for was directions to board a coach to the Panjab. Naj was still being harassed after five minutes of madness and arguments, pulling, tugging and threats. He grabbed his baggage and managed to break free.

Whilst searching for the bus station, Naj noticed a young woman in a similar situation. He couldn't help but get involved. It was hard to walk away after his own experience at the hands of the coolies. He went over and intervened. "Are they harassing you?"

"Yeah, this one won't let go of my bag," she said, pointing to a stocky little man with a red turban. Naj's face reddened with anger. He moved forward, grabbed her bag and threatened to stick his fist in the man's face. One of the men angrily said something to him in Hindi but the others dragged him away, leaving Naj and the girl looking at each other, relieved.

"Thank you for saving me! They were about to steal my bag."

"Are you Canadian or American?" he asked, noticing her accent.

"Canadian, actually," she answered smiling, which intrigued him. She paused for a moment. "First things first," she said, and held out her hand. "My name is Sonia, and yours?"

"Oh, I'm Naj," he replied.

"Pleased to meet you," she said with a smile.

"The pleasure is all mine," he replied with a wide grin. She was dressed casually in blue jeans and a T-shirt and large sunglasses rested on her head. She had beautiful almond-shaped eyes with straight jet black hair hanging half way down her back. She looked stunning. She stood out in the crowd and turned heads with her every move. Naj felt very attracted to her; there was a relaxed feeling between them.

"What shall we do now?" she asked.

"I need a cool drink myself, after all the pulling, tugging, arguing and everything else that has happened to both of us . . . would you like to join me?"

"Yeah, a cold drink would be nice," she said.

They picked up their baggage, walked over to a tea hut and purchased two bottles of ice cold Diet Coke. They sat in the shade sipping the drink as they talked, laughed and talked some more. It turned out that Sonia was also travelling to the Panjab to stay with her uncle and aunt; the first part

Dev Delay

of her Indian adventure. He could not believe it when she told him that her parents were also from Jalandhar, the same district as his Grandmother. She said that they had migrated to Ontario, Canada, in the early 1970s. She herself had been born and raised in Hamilton, a small town outside Toronto. She had graduated in media studies earlier in the year and decided to visit her ancestral home to take a well-earned break and learn a bit more about her heritage. This was her first visit to India and she planned to visit Kashmir, Tibet and Goa within a month before returning to start her new job with a media company based in Toronto. Naj was overwhelmed by Sonia's personality, smile, and accent.

The man at the tea shop directed them to the coach heading for the Panjab. They managed to purchase their tickets from the driver, and his assistant helped to put their luggage inside the compartment at the rear of the coach. They hurriedly took their seats in the half-empty coach. The impatient driver continuously revved the engine, causing thick black smoke to pour from its rear end. He gave the impression that they were about to leave at any second. His assistant touted around the coach bay looking for more passengers, but half an hour later they were still stationary with the engine roaring.

When the coach was jam-packed full of passengers, it began to reverse out of the bay. Naj popped his head out of the window and looked towards the back. The driver revved harder and the morning breeze blew the thick smoke from the exhaust into Naj's face, filling his lungs with fumes. He began to cough as others watched and passers-by laughed at him. The black smoke began to come in the window so the man sitting behind shouted at Naj to close the window and he did. His constant coughing brought tears to his eyes.

Sonia looked at him with concern: "Are you OK?"

Naj drank the last drop of water from his bottle to ease his coughing, pulled a tissue from his rucksack and wiped his face. Instead of cleaning it he made it dirtier, making him look like one of the dark-skinned locals. Sonia began to laugh hysterically at this. She covered her mouth with both hands, her eyes sparkling. Naj had no idea why. "What are you laughing at?" he asked, frowning. This made her laugh even louder.

"What's the joke?"

"Oh nothing, I'm just laughing." Her face reddened and tears ran as she continued to laugh louder and louder. She curled up with laughter. The passengers around them also began laughing. She pointed to his face with her index finger. "You've only been here for three hours or so," she said, "and you've already got a serious tan!"

"What, me?"

She took a small mirror from her makeup bag and handed it to him. He looked and began laughing. Naj's thigh touched Sonia's as they sat side by side, but she made no move to pull away.

The coach left the airport and began bumping along the uneven surface of the potholed road. It wasn't long before everyone settled down in their seats. The two women in front threw peanut shells on the floor, but no one seemed to mind; everyone did it. A guy sitting at the front suddenly began singing a song about India: "My India, I love my India, My beautiful India", and soon others joined him in the chorus. "We love our India," they kept repeating. No one complained; even the driver joined in with his waxed moustache twitching as his voice rose higher and higher. The passengers enjoyed the sing-song which lightened everyone's mood, but the driver's voice pierced Naj's ear drums. He couldn't believe that although the coach was packed like a sardine tin, was hot and sweaty, and he was struggling for breath, this idiot kept singing, "I love my India." How crazy was that?

Naj was a big guy with a healthy appetite; he had eaten everything given to him on the plane as well as consuming two bars of chocolate, a chicken sandwich, and two bottles of water. The bumpiness of the ride gave him a stomach ache and he bent over, holding his belly. Sonia leaned towards him. "What's the matter, Naj?" she asked. She could tell from his body language that he was in pain. She quickly passed him the bottle of water. He slowly straightened up again. She put the bottle to his lips and he took a small mouthful. For the next few minutes he sat in silence, curled up, then, in a panic, opened the window and vomited. There were bits of peas, tomatoes, meat and some yellow watery stuff; most of it got sprayed down the side of the coach. He sank back into his seat smelling like a box full of rotten eggs. Sonia gave him a paper towel from her rucksack and helped him clean his face and t-shirt.

"Are you alright now?" she asked. He nodded, then leaned back with his eyes shut and went to sleep. The early morning sun brightened the sky and the temperature began to rise. The engine roared and the coach accelerated on the open country road. Suddenly, a flash of smoke began to rise from underneath the bonnet of the bus. In an instant, the smoke turned into flames and closed over the bonnet and the windshield. The diver hit the brakes and the vehicle came to halt at the side of the road.

"Everybody out, out, out!" the driver shouted. A middle-aged woman with a small child on her lap began to scream hysterically, followed by others.

"Abandon ship!" someone shouted.

Naj was woken up by all the commotion and looked about. "What's going on?" he demanded.

Sonia had dropped off to sleep too, but now she was alert: "I don't want to worry you or anything; it's just that the flaming bus is on fire. I suggest you get your ass off the seat unless you're thinking about being barbequed for the locals," she said sarcastically, rising from her seat.

"Shit!" Naj jumped up in terror. "Let's get the hell out of here!"

The driver jumped out of the vehicle with a fire extinguisher in his grip. He drenched the bonnet in a great cloud of foam, and the fire was out. The crowd watched from a distance. They began to applaud him and he smiled. Luckily, no one was hurt and the excitement was over so far as the safety of the passengers and their luggage was concerned. Unfortunately, the bus was out of action and the only place it was going was the repair shop, on the back of a tow truck. The stranded passengers demanded a replacement or their money back. The driver was in no position to accommodate anyone but he reassured them that he'd spoken to the bus company and a replacement would take them to their destination first thing tomorrow morning. Of course, this was totally unacceptable and the frustrated passengers expressed their anger at the bus driver, who was used to this sort of thing. After about an hour, most of the passengers drifted away, leaving a few hardened ones still arguing their case.

Naj and Sonia managed to rescue their luggage from the bus after agreeing to wait until the morning and headed for a hotel some ten minutes walk down the road. A truck driver passing by sounded his horn at them.

"Kuttay da put!" Naj shouted back at him.

"Hey, you speak Panjabi?"

"One or two words, that's all," Naj admitted.

She let out a small exclamation of pleasure: "That's nice. I hope to pick up a few words while I'm here. My mother always said I should learn her tongue, but I didn't see the point. Besides, English is widely spoken across the globe, so it didn't seem important until recently when I became politically conscious. You know what? I kind of feel guilty for not listening to my mother. She had a point."

They had no trouble finding two separate rooms at the hotel. After a shower and change of clothes they found a table in the restaurant overlooking a car park.

"I'm going to order a beer and I could easily make that two if you like?" Naj asked with a smile.

Sonia liked him and felt totally comfortable in his company, so how could she refuse? "I haven't had a beer for months," she said, "but, yeah, let's see what the Indian beer tastes like." She would regret it when she woke early the next morning with a splitting hangover.

*

The afternoon sun glittered on the horizon. Sonia wore a white t-shirt neatly tucked into a tight hipster pair of dark jeans leaving her back and shoulders bare, her tanned skin smooth and silky. He was desperately trying not to come across as a pervert, but it wasn't easy with exuberant bosoms in his face. How could he miss them? An hour had gone by so quickly. They were on their third beer, and enjoying each other's company. Sonia talked about her college life, her friends and the guy she was in love with who suddenly turned religious, after which the relationship fell apart. She was finally over him after six months and there was nobody in her life at present. She went on to talk about her work and aspiration to become her own boss in the future, before settling down with a husband and kids.

Sonia was not a drinker. She liked an occasional wine rather than beer, but today she got the taste for beer, and kept up with her companion. Before long they were on their sixth bottle and the Indian beer was taking hold of her senses. The sun had gone down and the waiter had switched on the dim lights and turned the CD player on to play romantic songs and make the atmosphere cosier. Suddenly, Sonia looked deep into Naj's eyes. She reached across the table and placed her hand over his. Naj felt his stomach clench under the impact of those big dark eyes.

"I'm glad we've met, Naj," she said softly.

"Yeah, me too."

Except for the bartender, they had the room to themselves. It seemed completely natural that the two of them should continue. After all, they were on holiday. Sticking together made a lot of sense to both of them. But something was niggling at Naj. He kept thinking about Lucy. How would she react if she saw them together like this? Would she encourage it or slap him across his face?

"Let's order some food, shall we?" Naj asked.

"Yeah, you order and I need to visit the ladies'." Sonia had finished the last drop in her glass and struggled to stand up straight. He came to her rescue for the second time. Like a gentleman, he helped her to her feet. They stood facing each other and began to giggle. The bartender watched them from behind the counter with a wide grin. His smile got even bigger when Sonia leaned forward and placed her mouth over Naj's. His lips were warm and soft and she was enjoying herself. For a moment the bartender thought he was in a cinema watching an Indian movie. They kissed long and hard, not realizing someone was watching them.

The bartender decided to intervene. After all, they were in someone else's domain: "Would you like to order now or later, sir?"

They found themselves in an embarrassing situation. Sonia pulled away and her arm, which had been folded around Naj's neck, dropped to her side. She almost lost her balance in the process. She scrambled to her feet and tried heading towards the ladies', not knowing where to go.

"Yeah; can we order for the food to come up to our rooms?"

"Sir, no problem. You can make an order on the phone from your room." Naj took Sonia by the arm and led her upstairs at a dignified pace. They got to her door, but she had other ideas.

"You wouldn't leave a girl on her own in a strange place, would you?"

"Good night," he said, trying to pull away.

"Spoilsport! I thought you British were known for your sense of duty and adventure," she said with another kiss.

Naj accepted the challenge and followed her into the bedroom. The waiter waited for their order for food, but none came until six in the morning, when they requested two cups of strong coffee.

Naj and Sonia arrived early at the agreed bus stand and waited with the others. Naj felt a tinge of regret that he had slept with someone other than his true love, Lucy.

"What's the matter?" Sonia asked. "Your face looks as though you had seen a ghost or something."

"Oh, it's nothing, really. I blame it on the Indian beer."

"Yeah, you're right, it doesn't agree with me either. I'm feeling a bit funny in my stomach."

Journey Home

They piled the luggage onto the roof for the second time in two days and took their seats. The excitement of some passengers, especially the children, was intense. They were finally going home. Sonia slipped her hand into his and smiled at him.

"Let's hope this one doesn't break down like the last!" she said jokingly.

"No, have some faith, sweetie; this one looks in a better shape than the other. We'll be all right, trust me."

"Let's hope you're right, Naj. I'm losing valuable time."

Everyone sat and the driver revved up the engine. "Chaloo, chaloo," his assistant shouted from the rear of the bus.

"Last night wasn't a waste of time . . . or was it?" Sonia asked.

Naj glanced at her and gave her a peck on her cheek. "It was fun." Then his voice dropped slightly, with a tiny quaver. He turned quickly and looked onto a field where a herdsman was grazing his goats. Sonia never asked and he chose not to say anything about his girlfriend, Lucy, but she had a feeling he was probably seeing someone. She didn't care.

The bus picked up speed and they were silent until Naj said: "Did you say your auntie lives in Ludhiana?"

"Yeah, Ludhiana."

"We should be there in about four hours by my estimation."

"Yeah. I'm looking forward to seeing her. I'll spend a day or two there and then I'll travel down to Jalandhar to see a distant relative, an elderly lady. I've never seen or spoken to her but my mother says I must pay her a visit. She's in her nineties. After that I plan to spend a day at Amritsar and then head off."

"If you are in Jalandhar, come and see us."

"Yeah, I'll do that."

"Ring me first and I'll come and rescue you from the ancient woman you're talking about."

"You don't need to rescue me. She's nice and full of wisdom, my mother says."

Naj looked up into the sky. The clouds were brilliant silver against the blue: "I hope it rains and cool things down. It's too damn hot for my liking."

"Yeah."

Naj closed his eyes to get some rest and soon dozed off. Sonia too leaned back, eyes shut, listening to her favorite tune on her headset.

All conversation stopped when the driver suddenly hit the brakes in order to avoid a collision with an oncoming truck. He shouted something loudly in Panjabi and, in the blink of an eye, the two vehicles met head on in the middle of the road. There was no time for the passengers to do anything but scream because it happened so fast. The coach tossed and rolled over several times before ending up in a ditch, mangled and twisted. The engine was still running. Onlookers rushed to help. They tried to break the windows to get people out. It was total carnage. People were screaming for help, trying to escape. Many died instantly from the impact. Naj came to his senses, opened his eyes and realized what had happened. He looked at Sonia and saw that her face was bleeding from a cut on her forehead. In panic, he called out her name: "Sonia, Sonia, wake up!" There was no answer. She was unconscious. He realized the bus was on fire. "Shit, not again," he murmured. He looked about. *This is the end*, he thought. *Any minute now the coach is going to explode.* He tried to stand but he was trapped between the seats. He tried to pull himself free; it was no use. The reality of death crowded in on him. The end of a young life, never to see his Grandmother or Lucy or Mum and Dad, or laugh with Tom. He took a deep breath and struggled to free himself. Anyone who knows that their life is in imminent danger instinctively tries to better the odds by any means. Naj had his whole life in front of him and everything to live for. A protective survival mechanism took over. He had to save Sonia.

"It's going to blow up any minute!" someone shouted.

Naj grabbed Sonia by the arms and dragged her away from the flames. She was still unconscious. He checked her pulse; it was very faint and her breathing even fainter. She was barely alive. He felt helpless and could do nothing more than just hold her. "Give her water," someone said. He put a bottle of water to her lips and nothing happened. He felt angry with himself for nodding off. If he had been awake, he might have been of more use. The ambulance and the fire engine eventually turned up forty minutes after the crash. By this time a number of passengers who could have been saved had died. If only the medical help had come sooner! The strangers looked at each other and thought of the dead and their loved ones. Naj grabbed a doctor by the hand and begged him to save Sonia. She had lost a lot of blood. The doctor checked her pulse and her breathing. They put her in the ambulance and Naj held her hand as he prayed for God to save her. The coach exploded in flames and everyone ran for their lives. The remains of the coach and its cargo gradually turned into black ash. What mattered now was her life.

Naj's grip on her hand tightened as he told the doctor: "If she needs blood, please take mine, take mine. I'm healthy, young . . . take my blood." Tears were running down his muddy, bruised face and he kept repeating, "Please don't let her die; please don't let her die."

The doctor checked Sonia's breathing constantly as they drove to the hospital. She stopped breathing; there was no pulse. Her eyes were shut tight, her mouth was open, but she was gone. For the next few seconds, there was total silence. They all looked at each other in disbelief. There was nothing anyone could do now. Naj held her close. "You can't die on me now; we've just met," he said. He began to cry. He felt disgusted, angry, lonely and helpless. He would give anything to have her back sitting next to him, talking, smiling, and sharing her life story and adventures. Finally, he choked on the sadness as he sat there, dazed, holding her in his arms, her face bloodied and bones broken. He would always remember her as she had been. He paused and drew a deep breath. His face could not mask his sorrow. There was nothing anyone could say or do to relieve or comfort him.

CHAPTER TWO

Seven months had passed since Naj completed his BA honors degree in computer science at Middlesex University in London. Best friends since primary school, Naj and Tom had been spending a lot of time together since returning home.

Naj's graduation photograph hung proudly above the mantelpiece in the family's living room. A showpiece, so those who visited would be struck by it as soon as they entered. His mother, Jeeti, kept the portrait sparkling clean. This had become a daily ritual for her: she took pride in cleaning her most prized possession.

Her husband walked into the living room holding a cup of herbal tea. He stood by the window looking out, blowing on it.

"How many times have you cleaned Naj's photo since you got up this morning?" asked Darsh sarcastically. He was looking for a fight and his tone sparked it off. Jeeti broke into a cold sweat and responded with her usual solid defiance.

"Watch your tongue. Haven't you anything better to do than ask me useless questions?"

"What?" he asked, turning his head.

"I'll give you what!" she screamed back.

He spluttered his tea all over the window. "Damn," he said. Then he froze, with an audible intake of breath.

"Look what you've done, you clumsy old man!" Her body stiffened with rage. "I've just finished cleaning the window. You ought to be ashamed of yourself. A grown man who can't manage a cup of tea without spilling it all over the place," she said bitterly. She sucked in air, rushed to the kitchen, and returned with a handful of paper towels. "Now, move out of my way before I say something I might regret." Her voice rose with fury. She was dangerously near him now.

"But, but, let me explain . . ."

"I don't want to hear another word from you. Now move out of the way."

Darsh looked shaken up as he backed away nervously, regretting ever having come into the room. His eyes darted at her from a safe distance as she wiped the window, radiator, and floor.

"Men are totally useless, but this one tops them all," she murmured to herself.

"I heard that. That's not fair," he responded.

She cut him short. "*What's* not fair? You being sarcastic, or me cleaning your mess after you? Which is it? Come on, let's have it out." It was obvious she was exhausted and irritable and it was taking its toll on their relationship. She didn't know when to stop and continued to bark at him. "What's more, do I get so much as a 'thank you' from you? No, sir! Nothing of the kind, ever." She sniffed. The house dust got up her nose. She threw the duster on the floor as her face reddened. "All right, let's sort this out once and for all," she growled as she blew into her handkerchief. Her eyes were a startling red with allergy and anger. "Go find yourself another slave to do your cooking and cleaning. I've had enough of your verbal abuse and I ain't putting up with it anymore." The words came out in a racking sob.

"What?" said Darsh, as he looked at her in disbelief. His tongue got the better of him. "'Do what you have to do, you ungrateful woman,' he said, asserting himself, very much the man of the house now. He moved a step closer but kept his distance in case she lashed out at him, just as she had a few weeks back.

She just sat there sobbing with her face in her hands. He was as bad as she. The two of them fighting like cats and dogs.

"Where would you find another husband like me at your age, hey? What exactly is your problem?" He moved a step closer and squared up, pointing his index finger at her. She sneezed, almost catching him with a spray of mucous. "I mean, I provide *everything* for you, a roof over your head, food and clothing, everything. You're never short of anything, never. You have money in your purse and the fridge is always full of food, most of which gets thrown in the rubbish bin because you can't be bothered to use it before it starts to rot. Just think about all the starving people around the world. You of all people should know what it's like to be poor. You call yourself the perfect housewife. Pull the other one!" he blurted sarcastically.

She looked up at her husband for a long time, and then found herself laughing and sobbing uncontrollably at the same time, the tears flowing down her cheeks once more.

He was lost in his thoughts for a moment: *I married a Hindu devotee and she does puja daily. Hinduism teaches a wife to be respectful to her husband first and foremost but this one behaves the opposite. Then what is the use of puja rituals? Huh? What kind of Hindu woman is she? It's so confusing I fail to understand.* He looked at her feet. She wore odd socks and slippers that amused him. "Someone is going high-class," he murmured. He gazed out of the window at the grey skyline. At a distance, he could see a lone starling picking at the berries on a garden hedge. The weather didn't feel as cold as an English March.

"Maybe you should start paying me a little more respect. Because if it wasn't for me marrying you, you would probably be working away in some paddy field back in India, sowing rice all day with water up to your knees."

She straightened up as she removed a strand of hair from her face. "What do you mean?" Her voice was strained with a mixture of frustration and pain. She was not prepared to bear the brunt of Darsh's irrational anger for everything that had gone wrong in the house. She felt he should be grateful to her for bearing him a son, his heir. A son who was going to carry forward the family name. "Let me tell you something for nothing, my dear husband. The truth is that I rejected you at first glance when you came to my parents house with your bachola [go between] and mother. I remember when I came in with a tray of refreshments and saw you sitting looking at me from the corner of your eye. I didn't know who you people were. My mother just said, 'We have guests'. The words 'Uncle ji' almost came out of my mouth when I greeted you. You were not what I considered a young man, a boy. You had a full beard and looked much nearer my Dad's age than my own. I was shocked when my Mum told me the truth."

"Whatever." He shrugged and pressed the on button on the remote. The TV came on.

"Anyway, let's cut the story short. The truth is, of course, that I only agreed to marry you because I was put under enormous pressure by my family, including my father." Her voice began to tremble. "My mother, bless her soul, was on my side, but she was powerless and we had to go along with my father's wishes. He was the head of my family, and he always took the final decision. See; our only guilt was that we were poor and you agreed to waive your demands for a dowry. That was enough for my poor Papaji to give you my hand in marriage." She blew her nose in her handkerchief once more.

Darsh looked shocked. His eyes grew wide with disbelief and he stood shaking his head. His expression was still distressed when there was a knock on the door. He moved the curtain and saw the postman with a small package in his hand.

"Sign here," said the grumpy man at the door. The package had Darsh's son's name on it.

"It's for Naj."

"Leave it in the hall!"

Darsh was desperate for a way to avoid further confrontation. On the spur of the moment, he decided to take the parcel up to his son's bedroom. He was halfway up the stairs when he heard her yelling: "I said leave it in the hall! Come back here; I haven't finished with you!"

He sighed. He knew he was in more trouble than he bargained for. Sweat erupted on his forehead as though he had jogged five miles up the Baldock hills. He took a deep breath and did a u-turn. Avoiding Jeeti was no longer an option.

"On our wedding day," she began, "I cried like never before. My eyes were all puffed up and I looked more like a young widow who had just lost her husband than a blushing bride. Then, at night, you had the audacity to take my virginity. I never gave you permission. You animal, you raped me. I pleaded, I protested, and it all fell on deaf ears. I screamed with pain but you kept going until you were satisfied. A part of me died that night. I was hoping you would drop dead so that I could escape from underneath.

There were people in the house, but no one heard my screams. No one came to investigate or help. When you were done, you dropped off to sleep, grunting and snoring like a pig. I felt dirty and disgusted. I wanted to kill myself that night, but didn't know what to do or where to go. I just sat there and cried."

In the silence that followed, she had understood the new role of her wedded life and the curse that came with it.

Darsh reflected on her words, engulfed with shame. His head hung. He couldn't remember much of their wedding night given all the excitement of the day and the booze he had consumed that evening. It was way in the past, some twenty-seven years ago. *Why does she keep reminding me, punishing and tormenting me? I don't feel responsible as I don't even recall any of it. I was simply too drunk to remember anything.*

The move to the marital home had been traumatic for seventeen-year-old Jeeti. It meant a major displacement from her world of comfort and joy, where she had helped her mother with chores around the house and little else. She spent the rest of the time singing, dancing, and playing with friends in the neighborhood. Life was wonderful and, as fate would have it, all this changed with the blink of an eye. She was transformed from a carefree teenager to having the responsibilities of a respected wealthy man's wife.

"When I returned to my family home for a visit," Jeeti said, "I told my mother what you did to me and we cried together in each other's arms. My father, well he could see I was not happy. What could he say to me? After all, he sold my soul to you because we were poor. A man trading his young, innocent, loving daughter to another; the one he raised so tenderly. There was no other way out of poverty for us." She paused. "But what do *you* know about being poor and everything that comes with it? Your family always had money and lots of it."

"Nonsense," Darsh cut in, his anger dissolving in tolerant laughter. "You know very little about my family. Let me educate you about how we came up in the world to possess what we own today. We were poor like the rest of the village, with the exception of the money-lender. There were times when we had to face hardship too. Of course, we had a little bit more than some others, but nothing like what you call 'lots'." He fixed his gaze on her face. "See, my granddad was bold and adventurous, not afraid to try new things in an attempt to prosper. One day, he decided to try his luck in the Middle East, borrowed his passage fare from the money-lender and went off to Iran. He worked hard and sent everything he could save back to us. We soon paid off the borrowed money and, with the extra cash; we purchased the land around us. The value of the land had increased tenfold within five years. My granddad had clearly made a wise decision to invest his hard-earned money, and it certainly paid off for us financially. My Uncle Billa, Dad's older brother, was born idle and never did a day's work in his life. He got into drinking at an early age. It ruined his health, resulting in a premature death. He was only twenty-five. Then, when granddad passed away soon after, everything came to my father; the land, money, house, virtually everything. The rest is history."

*

Their marriage had improved a lot after the initial turbulent period. Jeeti, an able housewife even before she was married, took complete charge of running the house. Her mother-in-law was very impressed with her organizational skills and hard work. She was happy and relaxed now, as her daughter-in-law took over the household responsibilities. She handed over all the keys to the house except the key to the safe where she kept the cash and her jewelry, and that pleased Jeeti.

The first two years passed quickly. Darsh had gone to England and, as soon as he found employment and a place to live, he sent for Jeeti. Two or three months after arriving in England, Jeeti found herself pregnant with Naj. The family was overjoyed. Then came the dreaded news: Darsh's father died suddenly and Darsh turned to the bottle for comfort. Tempers flared as argument after argument took hold of the Dulaks.

*

Naj stepped into the room. There they were, his loving parents, at it again. Darsh, tall, dark and broad-shouldered with dark eyes, sat on the edge of the sofa. He was the one to whom Naj always looked for help and guidance. Jeeti, with high cheek-bones, light skin, and long black hair, stood by the fireplace and screamed at his father. Mum, his perfect role model; always calm and considerate, ready to offer advice and lend a helping hand. This was the first time that Naj had witnessed his parents engaged in a cat-and-dog fight, each holding their ground. He was surprised and shocked.

"Stop! What are you two fighting about?" He looked hard at both of them. "What's going on? Come on, would someone explain to me? I'm waiting."

"It's OK, son. It's nothing," said Darsh as he stood up. His hands were folded in front of him as though he were pleading before a magistrate.

"What you mean, 'It's nothing'? I could hear you shouting at each other as I came up the road." Naj was already distraught, since England had lost the match two to one. He felt that the referee had cheated and denied England the draw that they deserved. The game had been fresh on his mind as he walked home from the pub. He was already in a foul mood. "Why can't you live like other people and be nice to each other and learn to resolve things rationally and sensibly?"

"It's your father!" Jeeti complained, pointing at Darsh.

"Me? I didn't start it," said Darsh, raising his voice.

Naj butted in: "I don't care *who* started it; I want both of you to stop this nonsense at once." His eyes were bright with anger, his voice raised. "Do you hear me?"

Shaken, Darsh and Jeeti glared at each other, not knowing what to say or do.

"Shall I make you something to eat?" Jeeti asked to defuse the situation, while Darsh began to fidget with a magazine on the coffee table. No one answered and the room fell silent.

Naj picked the remote control off the coffee table and turned up the volume. There was a knock on the door, and they all looked at each other.

"I'll get it," said Naj.

"I wonder who that could be?" Jeeti asked. Darsh just stood and shrugged. They both listened intently as the door opened. They recognized Tom's voice, but were unable to make out what was being said. All they heard was a phrase: "It's not a good time right now, bruv." After a few seconds, they heard the door close.

"Who was it?" Jeeti asked.

"No one, mother," Naj replied, and went upstairs to his bedroom. *Why wouldn't they tell me what they were arguing about?* He thought. He was disappointed in them; they should know better at their age. *Maybe they're going through a mid-life crisis; couples in middle age do.* He felt remorseful and was disappointed at himself for telling them off like children. He felt he should have had more control over his anger. He had forgotten the word 'respect' and was angry. Naj turned the CD player on and lay on the bed with his hands behind his head listening to U2's "It's a beautiful day." *Maybe I was a little harsh on my parents; all couples argue from time to time,* Naj thought as he looked at the ceiling. After a while, when he heard them laugh, he felt at ease. It was perfect, as it had always been. He had been born to a wonderful woman and a father of whom he was proud. They were two lovely human beings with a beautiful house in a good neighborhood. Life couldn't be better. Naj turned on his side and fell asleep.

Later that evening, Naj went off to his local leaving his parents alone in the kitchen. Jeeti couldn't help raising the subject once again and snarled at her husband: "Cleaning the house is *my* job, it's my domain, it is my business and I don't need *you* to interfere with any of it, do you hear me?"

"Don't start that again, please, I beg you," he pleaded. "I haven't recovered from your earlier onslaught."

Jeeti was still full of anger and there was no stopping her: "The fact is, you always criticize me whenever I'm dusting or cleaning. Would you prefer to live in a pigsty? If I want to clean my son's portrait ten times a day then I will do it. I don't need your approval."

"All right, do what you want, I don't care. One thing is for sure; I'm not going to argue with you ever again," Darsh retorted.

"Thank you. I will do whatever pleases me from now on. Besides, you never offer to help me even when I'm run down or unwell, do you? You just sit there reading your Panjabi paper demanding things of me as if I'm your servant or something."

Darsh sat down on the settee, distraught and confused, his heart bleeding with pain and anger. *What did I do to deserve this woman, for Christ's sake?* He thought. He removed his spectacles, wiped his eyes, walked over to the drinks cabinet, pulled out a half full bottle of rum, poured it into a glass, drank the lot in one go and refilled it.

"You always do that, it's the same every time, always turning to the bottle for help, instead of facing up to the problem and finding a solution. I blame my father for finding a weak husband for me. Other women have strong, courageous and loving husbands and I ended up with you, a drunk, useless lay about. If they were alive today, what they would say I daren't even think!" Darsh sat, listening to every word, his head in his hands, staring at the floor without saying anything. He wondered if he'd been cursed to have ended up with a hot-tempered woman like Jeeti. *She used to be so loving and kind! I don't know what's happened to her lately. I don't know what to make of her anymore. One minute she's all fine, and then she turns into a werewolf and attacks me. Mood swing after mood swing. It's beyond me. I can't take anymore.* He took another sip. *The woman is going mad*, he thought. He was battling with his feelings valiantly and getting nowhere, becoming more miserable by the minute.

She came and stood over him: "You didn't hear a word I said, did you?"

Darsh sat and stared at the bottle in front of him. He hadn't wanted this to happen. *There's no point to any of this,* he thought. He was helpless.

"Why don't you answer me, have you suddenly lost your tongue?" she cried. It seemed that frustration had got the better of her.

Darsh controlled his pain and frustration by showing restraint. Somehow, he had the impression that Jeeti had no idea what was happening or the impact this was having on their relationship. She seemed oblivious to everything he was feeling.

"Give me that bottle, I'm going to empty the damn thing down the sink!" she screamed. Darsh tried to reach for the bottle but Jeeti beat him to it.

Darsh felt miserable. *I don't know what to say to her. It's not fair, she has no right to take away my drink and waste it just like that. Why take it out on the bottle?* He sipped the last drop from his glass and considered that he had ignored her intimidating tactics. He had avoided her sharp tongue and done everything he could, except facing her head on. There was no point in fuelling her anger, and if he had, it would only have resulted in making it worse for the family. *Besides,* he thought, *she'll be back to her normal self in a few hours.*

Almost a whole day passed without a word from either of them. Normally they shared an evening meal, prepared by Jeeti of course, but her mind was still occupied with earlier events and she was not in the mood for cooking. Although Darsh kept hoping for a hot meal, in the end he settled for a packet of crisps and a beer.

Jeeti turned in for the night just after ten, an hour earlier than usual, followed by her husband some thirty minutes after. They slept in silence, each sticking to their own side. Their bodies did not come into contact, hardly moving or turning. Each reflected on their own actions before finally dropping off to sleep.

Next morning, when Darsh woke, he heard Jeeti shuffling around in the kitchen. Then came the clinking of crockery and the smell of fresh coffee wafted into his nostrils. He heard her footsteps coming up the stairs. She pushed the door open with her foot and entered the room, holding a tray. "Are you awake?" she asked as she deposited the tray on the bedside cabinet. Darsh slowly turned over towards her, rubbing his eye with the palm of his hand.

"What time is it?" he asked.

"It's gone nine."

He sat and pulled himself up, resting his back on the headboard. She handed him his coffee as if nothing had happened the day before. That's how it was between them: One minute they were at it, trying to inflict pain on each other, and then a few hours later, there was harmony once more.

"How is it on the weather front this morning?" he said, sipping his coffee.

She glanced towards the window. "Oh, it's not bad. It looks as if the sun is trying to come out."

"Fancy going for a walk on the common, dear?"

"It's a nice thought, but I've got tons of housework to be getting on with. You go on your own and I'll make you breakfast on your return."

He smiled before putting the cup to his lips: "What time did Naj come back from the pub last night, darling?"

"I'm not sure; I did hear the door open and close, but didn't check the time."

"Are you going to say anything to our son?"

"About what?"

"About coming in late, of course."

"No, I don't think so. He's a grown-up now. Have you forgotten about yesterday when he spoke to us both in that parental tone?" said Darsh with a worried expression. The thought of confronting Naj about his late nights terrified him. *What if he was furious with me, how would I deal with that? And what might lie ahead for him in the future?* He couldn't take that chance. He was relieved when she told him she spoke to her son, although he thought he probably should do so too.

For the next few minutes they sat in the bed, silent, hardly moving. The clock ticked away, tick, tock, tick, tock . . .

"You all right?" asked Darsh softly.

"Yes, are you?" she replied.

He apologized and said that he was tired.

"Me too."

"I didn't mean to upset you yesterday," said Darsh, following another silence.

"It's OK, but don't make a habit of it," Jeeti replied, as if to prove a point.

Darsh realized where this was going so he quickly changed the subject.

*

Jeeti and Darsh were very proud of their son's academic achievements and loved to talk about them, mostly in the evening and weekends when they were relaxing together. Relatives and other visitors to the house were also told of their Naj's achievements and the same topic was repeated a number of times, usually to the same people, who out of respect pretended to be hearing it for the first time. In fact, they were bored with hearing the whole thing repeated time and again from the Dulaks.

"Did you see Aunty Flora's face when she looked at Naj's graduation photo?" asked Jeeti, as she stitched a button onto a shirt.

"No. What happened to her face?"

"She put on a happy face but underneath all that make-up you could tell she was burning with jealousy."

"You shouldn't take any notice of her. She is a jealous, sad old woman. She just can't help it."

"Stupid cow, that's what she is if you ask me." She looked at Darsh to gauge his reaction. "Ouch!" she cried.

"What happened?"

"I just pricked myself with the stupid needle; that's what happened." She grabbed the shirt and threw it at him in frustration. "Sew the button yourself, it's your shirt," she said, putting the injured finger to her lips.

Darsh picked the shirt off the floor. *Here we go again*, he thought. He loved his wife very much and cared for her deeply, but felt anger towards her when she suddenly threw a tantrum at him without a reason. He couldn't bear it. The thought of reaching out to her was far, far from his mind. He walked out of the room with the shirt in his hands. *So now what?* He thought. *I'm not going to condemn myself for feeling the way I do about her right now, angry and frustrated.*

Naj was the only one in their extended family who had studied at university. They were so proud. An hour later they were in the living room and she raised the subject again, as she glanced with pride over to Naj's degree certificate.

"What qualification do you need to be a Prime Minister?" Jeeti asked her husband.

"I'm not sure. Why do you ask?"

Dev Delay

"I would like our son to go into politics. Maybe he can become the first Asian Prime Minister of this country."

"That's a wonderful thought, darling. H'm, my son the Prime Minister, that would be something. What was the name of the queen who ruled India?"

"Queen Victoria."

"Are you sure? I thought her name was 'Queen Gloria'."

"I'm sure it was Queen Victoria."

"It always sounded like 'Gloria' to me, but never mind, like they say one learns something new every day."

"Yes, darling, if you say so."

"Just think for a minute. If Naj became a Prime Minister of England then we Indians could return the favor."

'Naj isn't Indian, darling, he's English. He was born here, remember; it's his parents who are Indian, you and me."

From the day Naj was born it had always been their wish and aspiration for their only son to be educated in the United Kingdom, preferably Oxford or Cambridge, so that they could show off to their neighbors, relatives, and the rest of the world that their son had attended the same university as the likes of Mahatma Gandhi and Pandit Nehru. In reality, Naj was not gifted with the intelligence or brain power of either Gandhi or Nehru. He had always found academic studies boring and difficult. In fact, he was not academic at all. He struggled all the way through from primary to secondary school as well as with his A-levels.

"Naj come and have a look son."
"What Mom."
"Come and see this."

"I'm watching Karina Kapoor's latest movie. Your Grandmother loves her to bits. She a brilliant actress?"

"What do I know about Indian cinema, actors and actresses? You know I don't watch Indian films. I find them so boring. The story line is always the same, boy girl, girl boy; lots of singing, dancing, merry-making and crying. Don't the story writers know anything else to write about?"

"What's your problem? Isn't that what life is all about? Falling in love, falling out of love, joy of love, singing, dancing, romancing . . . these are some of the good things in life; the rest of it is quite boring, don't you think?"

"Mother, where have you been all your life? Don't you know anything other than just Indian films? You amaze me with your comments, you really do. It seems to me that you've lived a sheltered life."

She was disappointed with him. *Why is he trying to annoy me?* She thought. *He used to annoy me when he was going through his adolescence, I could understand that; and now at his age for heaven's sake. How can he accuse his mother of not knowing much? Who does he think delivered him and made him what he is today?*

"Well, let me tell you, it wasn't your father, it wasn't the Prime Minister nor was it Santa Claus, it will surprise you to know, and actually it was this woman who made many sacrifices in order for you to tell her that she does not know much other than Indian films!" She threw her hands in the air and burst into tears, weeping openly.

Naj leant forward and tried to put his arms around her to console her, but she pushed him away and he felt abandoned, like a newborn abandoned by its mother. He apologized and pleaded for forgiveness. She got up, crossed to the fireplace and stood with her back to him, blowing her nose into a handkerchief. The door opened and his father walked in.

"What's going on?"

Jeeti looked up at him with tears on her face, and he was concerned for her.

"Oh it's nothing, Dad, nothing at all."

She wiped her face and blew again into a handkerchief and then looked at him, wondering if she should say something, but instead she left the room.

"What do you mean 'nothing'? Why is your mother crying then?" he asked, wondering if it would lead to confrontation with his son. He couldn't afford to drive a wedge between the two of them. He was relieved when Naj explained word for word what had happened between him and his mother.

"In her eyes I probably behaved badly, but I did apologize straight away, Dad," Naj protested.

"OK, not to worry, she'll be all right in a little while. Leave it to me. I'll talk to her."

*

The three year degree course wasn't easy for Naj; once again he struggled all the way through and at the end just managed to scrape through with help from his friends and the internet. His parents were none the wiser. They had no concept of the English education system. They could hardly read or write English themselves. They relied solely on their son's information with respect to matters of education. Naj was smart, streetwise and manipulative in getting his way around his parents, especially his mother; in her eyes, he could do no wrong. She was the one who held the key to the family's purse. He knew what it took and always got his way when it came to getting money out of her. His father, on the other hand, was very tight with money.

On one occasion, Naj told his parents that both Cambridge and Oxford had offered him a place, but he didn't wish to study there because all his friends were going to Middlesex and he too would be happy to go there. Obviously, they were very disappointed that he did not choose the internationally renowned universities where some of the most important and distinguished people in the world had studied. They tried telling him the importance of being educated at one of the best universities in the world and attempted to bribe him with a gift of a car, holidays of his choice, and designer clothes. Naj's closest friend, Tom, was also asked to help change his mind. Both of them had a good laugh at their local when Tom told him what Naj's parents had asked him to do. His mother took it badly and was prescribed anti-depressants to cope with the disappointment; she made herself sick and often cried herself to sleep.

"My old man and old lady don't know anything about English education, right," Naj said to Tom as they drank in their local, "and they're on my case all the time, pushing me towards Cambridge and Oxford; they're driving me up the wall!"

"Why don't you tell them the truth and be done with it?"

"No. I can't do that, that'll break my old lady's heart."

"So . . . what's your plan Dr. Who?"

"I don't know. I'll think of something."

Naj's parents could not get him to change his mind. In the end it was too much and they finally gave in. What could they do other than fully support their God-given gift, their only child, their only son, the heir to the throne, the one who was going to carry forward the name of their family? Richard Jones, their next door neighbor, who worked for the social services, told them on one occasion that, "children are like a bar of soap; if one tried too hard to press them, they could slip away altogether from underneath." Naj was their only child and their lives had revolved around him from the day he was born. Life without him was not even worth thinking about, so they avoided making a mistake that would jeopardize their relationship with him.

"He's so stubborn and does whatever takes his fancy. What about *my* feelings? After all, I'm only his mother, for God's sake," said Jeeti in frustration.

"He's English, what do you expect from him? The English culture has taught him to put himself above everyone else. As far as he's concerned he's doing nothing wrong, and I suppose it's normal for him to behave in that manner," said Darsh.

"I think it's wrong. He should think about our feelings too, especially on a major issue such as choosing the right university."

"I agree with you a hundred percent, but you know your son. If we press him too hard he may leave home altogether and then what?"

"I know, I know, I can't bear the thought."

Naj was excited about securing a place at the University of Middlesex and looked forward to moving out of the family home. He thought about the total freedom away from his parents, including the ability to come and go as he pleased, to go to bed late and play his rock music loud.

"I'm going to have a ball when I move into my digs in London," he said to Tom in the pub.

"You lucky bastard. I wish I was coming with you, mate."

Journey Home

"London isn't a million miles away, is it? It's only a thirty minute ride on the train. Come down at the weekend; you can organize the booze and I'll ask some birds to come from Uni."

"Yeah, sounds cool, man. I'm always up for a laugh, you know that, bruv."

"You want another?"

"No. I'd better not. I've got be up early in the morning for my milk rounds."

"Right then, drink up; we're off."

Naj rented a room in a shared house North of London. The landlord, Mr. Ali, a Bengali, was a shrewd businessman. He went out of his way to target new out-of-town students each academic year, so as to maximize the profits from his property. He was acutely aware that these students didn't ask many questions and, from past experience, he knew that their parents were often prepared to pay the asking price. Besides, the demand for a private let on the open market for the right price in London was high. Newcomers to the capital paid dividends for the likes of Mr. Ali and he loved going smiling to the bank with their cash.

The shared let was close to Turnpike Lane Underground station. It was an average sized terraced four-bed roomed property. There were three rooms on the first floor and the fourth room on the ground floor was originally the living room. Naj's room was the smallest; a high-ceilinged room on the first floor, with a big Georgian-style sash window that overlooked the garden and a graveyard at the back, making him feel uncomfortable. He had no choice in the pecking order; all the other rooms were taken before he arrived. It was the only vacant room available within his means. Although his room was the smallest, it had the minimum of furniture: a single bed with a firm mattress, a small dresser, and a wardrobe. The landlord asked for three months' deposit up front. At ninety five pounds per week, this wasn't cheap. His Mum and Dad took care of the finances and helped him move in a week before the starting date of his course.

Naj had already met John and Maggie, two of his three house-mates. The third, Jenny, was away visiting her parents and John told him that she would return in the next few days. He was looking forward to meeting her. Maggie told him that she was on the same course as him. John Doherty was from Belfast. He had moved in just over two weeks before, and was enrolled on a history course. John and Maggie suggested a house-warming party and Naj thought it would be cool. Maggie phoned Jenny and she was up for it too.

Naj was quick on the phone to his mate Tom "What are you doing next Saturday, mate?"

"Not much. What's up?"

"You fancy coming down to London?"

"Yeah, that'll be cool, man."

"We're organizing a little party at my flat. Make sure you bring a bottle or two, right?"

"No problem, you leave that to me; I take it you got some chicks coming."

"Yeah, yeah, no worries."

"Sweet. See you Saturday, man . . ."

John had been a DJ back in Belfast and he agreed to take care of the music side of things. He loved his music and a pint of Guinness.

"I'll take care of the food as long as you all chip in," said Maggie.

"Yeah, that's great; thanks for that."

"I'll take care of the security," said Naj. "And that leaves Jenny to do the clearing and cleaning up afterward. Everything sorted."

Maggie preferred to be called 'Madge' rather than her real name. Her pop favorite, Madonna, was referred to as Madge. A Geordie lass, she was from a village called Detters End near Newcastle and was a student of Art and Design on a three year degree course. Her Mum and Dad ran their own vehicle hire business and considered themselves reasonably well off. She had only moved in just over two weeks earlier. This was the first time she had been away from her family. She felt vulnerable and was missing them already. At first, she had also been very excited about moving into her own space, but the novelty of life in the big smoke soon wore off. The thought of transferring to another university near her home had entered her mind more than once. She missed her mother who called her several times a day and told her daughter to stick it out for a few more weeks before abandoning London.

Naj considered his lodgings very shabby and felt the house would benefit from a lick of paint. When Mr. Ali dropped in to fix a leak in the kitchen sink, Naj took the opportunity to confront him, but ended up saying much more than he should have about the state of the house. Mr. Ali responded angrily by telling him that he only rented him the room because he felt duty-bound, he being one of his own kind, an Asian. He also told him that if he did not wish to stay there then he should consider looking elsewhere. He went on to say that there were many people who would be willing to give their right arm for a room in this location. Naj was aggrieved but wisely refrained from asking further questions. The conversation ended and Naj's face was filled with anger as he walked upstairs to his room with his tail between his legs. He was learning fast about life in the big city and about himself.

*

The Dulak family lived in a small village called Delcock in Hertfordshire. Naj had been born prematurely at thirty-two weeks, weighing a mere three pounds, seven ounces. The medical staff at the Lister Hospital in Stevenage had been very concerned about his health, in particular his lungs, and it was touch and go for a while for him. He was unable to breathe on his own and was put on a ventilator immediately. For the following six weeks, his home was the incubator in the maternity ward and he was under the care of Dr. Gura. Prior to his birth, Jeeti had begun to lose blood and had been admitted to the hospital for fear of losing her and the baby's life. The medical staff monitored her progress and she gave birth a week later by Caesarean. The pregnancy had been difficult and complicated all the way through and Dr. Gura had to remove her cancerous ovaries immediately after his birth. The news devastated the Dulaks, who had planned on having a large family.

Naj's tiny frame soon gained weight and after two months he was allowed home. His parents and their extended family were all overjoyed by his arrival. In India, his Grandmother Jawali celebrated his birth by handing out ladoos and payrhays to the poor in her neighborhood and her close relatives and neighbors were all sent a box of special methaee from the 'Sangha Sweets' shop in Jalandhar. The Dulaks hired the village community centre and celebrated Naj's birth with food, music and a children's entertainer with their neighbors and relatives.

Journey Home

Naj grew fast and spent much of his time after school playing football with his mates on the village green, going to the cinema, fishing and doing the kind of things boys did at his age. Life was good to him and he considered himself one of the locals. Even though his parents spoke with a different accent and ate food with their fingers it didn't matter; they were his family and he loved them dearly.

Darsh and Jeeti had come to England from Panjab, India, in 1970, initially staying with relatives in Southall for a month and then moving to Hertfordshire for work. Naj felt at home in Hertfordshire. All his friends were here, so why shouldn't he? He had the same right as everyone else to call this place his home. There were no other Asian families in the village and little knowledge of Asian culture or traditions. All Naj's friends were white and they all thought the world of him. He was a talented football player and played in the Sunday League with the village team. He even had trials with Arsenal and Southampton. Both clubs were interested in signing him until he broke both his legs in a car accident at the age of fifteen. They told him that they would look at him again when he resumed playing. It was almost a year before he played and he never recaptured his earlier form. Naj had his sights set on becoming a professional footballer from an early age; that was now gone out the window forever. He was devastated. Many months went by before he finally accepted the reality of his situation. His dream of a career playing football at the highest level and playing for England was shattered.

*

Naj had been taking a much-needed rest after all the hard work he had put into his degree course over the last

Dev Delay

three years. He wasn't in any hurry to find a job, or to do anything else for that matter. Since completing his studies, his daily life had become unstructured and he only engaged in things when he felt like it. His priorities were different now, so far as he was concerned. He did things as he pleased. He was often down at his local with his mates drinking late into the night. At home he watched TV and DVD's until the early hours and then went to bed, often sleeping late into the afternoon. Sometimes he had only just got out of bed before his Mum and Dad returned from work in the evening. His mother would cook for him with pride but he preferred takeaways. Throwing away his food upset his parents no end. There had been arguments when he told his mother not to cook for him without checking with him first but she still cooked for him regardless. His parents found it hard to cope with his challenging attitude and his drop-out hippie lifestyle since his return from university. They thought a change of environment might be the solution for them all. A visit to his Grandmother in India could be the answer for the whole family. The experience of spending time in India might help him to change his outlook on life. His Grandmother had been asking for him since his birth, and it made sense for him to spend some time with her.

Initially, Naj was not interested in going to India, but he came around to the idea after talking it over with his friend Tom and Lucy, Naj's girlfriend. His parents paid for his flight and gave him five hundred pounds to spend. They packed his chili-red suitcase, which was stuffed to bursting with his own clothes and presents for his Grandmother Jawali, his distant Begumpur wali Massi, and other relatives.

Naj looked at the suitcase bursting at the seams. "Who's gonna carry this?" he asked. "It weighs a ton."

"It's only your clothes and some presents for your Grandmother," Jeeti replied innocently.

"My clothes? My clothes don't weigh that much. I'm only taking two pairs of jeans and a few t-shirts; that's all. Open the suitcase and let me see what's in it!" Naj demanded.

The phone rang. Darsh answered: "Hello, who is it?" Then, "It's for you, Naj."

"Who is it?"

"It's Tom."

"Tell him I'll phone him back. No . . . Dad, on second thoughts let me talk to him."

Darsh looked at Jeeti angrily. "I told you not to stuff the suitcase with your old clothes! Who's gonna wear them, your Begumpur wali Massi?"

"My old clothes are not for her, they're for the poor. Mata ji will distribute them amongst the needy. I phoned her last week." She drew a long breath. "I don't know what's the matter with him. He's allowed to take twenty-five kilos, that's not too much to ask, is it?"

"Just take out one or two items, that'll calm him down."

CHAPTER THREE

Naj arrived at 10 Rastoorba Nagar, his Grandmother Jawali's bungalow, two days after the coach crash. He stood by the iron gates on the path leading to the house. A thin, black stray dog prowled nearby. When he looked again, it had vanished into a shadow without a trace. *That's strange,* he thought, *what's going on?*

There was no doorbell to press or knocker to knock. He looked over the gate but there was no sign of life. He wondered if anyone was in the bungalow. He bent down, picked up a small stone and banged the gate with it. No one answered. A warm breeze rustled the bush behind the gate. He banged a little harder and waited anxiously, eyes fixed on the front door. Again, no one responded.

Mum and Dad did say they were going to phone Grandma to let her know that I was coming. I hope they didn't forget, he thought. He advanced and called out "Grandma, it's me, Naj. Open the gates please." Almost instantly a small, skinny man with a slightly crooked nose, wearing a white vest and khaki shorts, appeared from the side of the house. He walked up the garden path to the gate as if he himself was the master of the house. He stared at Naj with beady eyes. "Who are you?" he asked suspiciously.

"Hello," said Naj. "Could you tell me if Mrs. Dulak is in the house?"

"Who wants her?"

"Her grandson."

"Where is he?"

"You are looking at him."

This amused the little man: "You are having a laugh."

"No. Could you go get her for me?"

"Go away."

Naj felt like a child who had been smacked for being naughty. He was sure he was at his Grandmother's bungalow. The shadow deepened on the patio by the banana tree. A cat came and brushed against the man's leg and then disappeared under a bush. Confused, Naj checked to reassure himself and looked at the house number on the gate. It was 10. He then walked to the end of the street; the sign stated Rastoorba Nagar. He was now a hundred and ten percent sure that the house with the iron gates was truly his grandma Jawali's house. He returned to the gate and saw the same thin black dog staring at him from a distance. *How strange*, he thought. The little man was still in the front garden smoking a cigarette. Naj was amazed at his attitude and arrogance. Every person he'd had dealings with here seemed to have this authoritative attitude. *I don't know why that is. Maybe it's us British who are to blame for that colonial arrogance*, he thought.

"Excuse me, sir," said Naj politely. The man gave him a mean look, threw the cigarette away and marched towards him.

"I told you to go away, now go!" he said in a raised voice. His deliberate turning away made it clear that he was snubbing him. Naj persisted and continued to pursue him, asking: "Can you tell me if Mrs. Dulak lives here?"

"Are you deaf as well as stupid? I told you before to get lost and you are not taking any notice. So tell me, what's wrong with you? Now clear off. I won't tell you again."

Dev Delay

Naj stood rooted to the spot. He wasn't getting anywhere, despite all his protests about his identity. He was thinking about what he could do next, but was damned if he was going to be stopped from going through the gates of his rightful ancestral home.

Suddenly, on hearing raised voices, Mrs. Datta, the next door neighbor, arrived on the scene. She wore a floral salwar-kameez. Her shoulder-length jet black hair was a mess.

"What's the problem, Ramu?" she asked the little man.

"It's OK, Mrs. Datta, I can handle this on my own."

She turned to Naj: "What's your business here? Who are you anyway?"

Naj gave Mrs. Datta a sidelong glance and said: "My name is Naj and I'm Mrs. Dulak's grandson from England. This man won't let me through the gate, and I don't know what to do to convince him. I've asked him to inform my Grandmother several times and he refused. He's not listening to me."

Mrs. Datta looked over him. Her expression was curious but doubtful.

"Please believe me, lady. My name is Naj. I am who I say. Why would I lie? There's no reason. I am Naj, son of Darsh and grandson of Jawali Dulak." His voice was quiet, his eyes direct. "I'm telling you the truth."

"I don't believe you. You could be making all this up and, besides, just look at yourself." She turned up her nose. "You look and smell like a rubbish collector. How do you explain that? Show some proof of who you are."

Ramu grinned, spreading his shoulders, making himself look bigger than he actually was.

A crashing sound from the garden startled her. "Uh-huh. What the hell was that?" said Mrs. Datta. She feared the worst and rushed to investigate. She wasn't surprised when she found a stray dog licking the remains from a broken clay pot on the ground. "Damn these stray dogs!" she murmured. "You can't leave anything out in the open for a second. This is the third time in a month I had my pots broken by the same dog. I've reported it to the municipal board a number of times and you know what, nothing, they don't do anything. I don't know why I pay my taxes to them." The dog jumped over the wall on seeing her grab a stick and ran off.

Naj stood, frustrated and sidelined. It was a beautiful morning, but not for him. Mrs. Datta returned to Naj with the stick in her hand, cursing the dog. The mean expression on her face was worthy of a glossy Indian women's magazine; firm, confident and business-like.

"Now, where was I?" she said, looking at Naj. "Ah yes, let me see your ID or something, otherwise clear off."

Naj moved back a step staring at the stick, his frustration deepening. He feared for his personal safety at the hands of this madwoman, who was waving a stick at him. Her behavior shocked him, the hairs on his neck stood on end. *She's fucking trouble,* he thought.

The little man took a step forward, spurred on by Mrs. Datta, his shadow scudding across the path behind him. Naj looked at him and saw anger in his eyes.

Why doesn't she believe me, for Christ's sake? Naj thought. *What's with this stick, anyhow? Is she serious about her threat to attack me? If she is, what will I do? Run away or defend myself?*

Naj quickly reached into his back pocket and pulled out his passport, which was damaged and soiled. "That's me, there, that's my picture, you can see this is me," he said, pointing to his passport photo. The little man moved closer, his eyes glued to the document. He had never seen a passport in his life, never mind owning one. Mrs. Datta held his passport and inspected it, flicking pages, one after another. She looked at its thick dark red cover, front and back, then at his photo closely, then looked at him, and once again at the photo, as if she was an expert in immigration matters. The passport was genuine. He was telling the truth. She agreed with it. *So what happens now?* She wondered. *I must make amends and apologize to the poor boy. I have made a mistake, stupid old me.*

"Harey Ram, yes, yes, it is you," she said with a smile, instantly putting her arms around him, hugging him as if he was her own long-lost son. Naj was relieved. She turned to Ramu, who was slinking away from them, back to the house in order to avoid Mrs. Datta's sharp tongue.

"Ramu!" she shouted. He stopped dead on hearing her. He stood rooted and stared at the ground, afraid to face her. His face wore the expression of a man condemned to the gallows. He wondered if this was the end for him. A youth walked by, nodding his head, music trickling out of his iPod.

"Come here, haramzaday, come and explain yourself," she said furiously. Ramu shuffled slowly towards them with his head bowed, his tail between his legs. *I'm fated to live my life in misery,* he thought. "What have you got to say for yourself?" she asked in a raised voice. Ramu tried to answer, his tongue numb with fear. All that came out was a grunt and then, with difficulty, he murmured something in a very low tone.

"I didn't hear you. Speak up." He stood there shaking.

"I . . . I didn't recognize him, madam. I really didn't," he protested. She moved closer and grabbed his ear. She gripped tightly and began to twist. It felt like the heft of a butcher's knife. Pain sliced into Ramu's head and he screamed.

"Did that hurt?" she asked sarcastically and gave it another half twist before he could answer. His mouth opened wide and the yell could be heard a mile away.

"Please, Mrs. Datta, stop, stop, before you tear my ear off!" She looked down on him.

"You've always pretended to be brave-hearted, but you've turned out to be a little lamb! Ha, ha, Ramu is a little lamb!" she taunted. "What are you?"

"I'm a little lamb, madam."

"That's right, you are a little lamb. Now tell me, do you recognize this young man?" she shouted at him again. Naj could see from her expression that she was enjoying herself.

"Yes . . . yes, yes, madam, I am very sorry madam, I have made a big mistake, please forgive me."

"It's not me you should be apologizing to; it's this young man. He's mata ji's grandson, Naj." She let go of his ear and he almost fell to his knees. Naj was appalled by Mrs. Datta's actions and almost intervened in order to stop her, but had to remind himself that this wasn't the right time.

Ramu felt his ear gingerly to see if it was still attached to the side of his head. He knelt at Naj's feet.

"Please, sir, have mercy on me. I didn't know who you were. I thought you were a beggar or something," he said, with tears in his eyes. Naj looked at himself. His clothes were torn, smelly and dirty. He hadn't taken a shower since leaving England. Even Mrs. Datta had taken him for a local beggar.

"Please, Auntie ji, please don't say a word to Mata ji, I beg you; I'll do anything, anything you want me to, anything at all, she'll throw me out," cried Ramu.

"Who is this man?" Naj asked Mrs. Datta.

"Him? Well, his name is Ramu and, believe it or not, he works for your Grandmother. In essence, he is your servant."

"Wait a minute, my servant? What do you mean?" It was an innocent statement of fact, Ramu was his family's servant, but Naj felt uncomfortable with the word "servant". *We don't have servants back home*, he thought.

"He looks after your Grandmother and takes care of things around the house, from cooking, cleaning, gardening, painting to carrying and fetching; anything and everything."

Naj stared at Ramu who stood in front of him. Ramu dropped his face to the ground. He began to shake and tears ran down his face. He was remorseful, and wished he was somewhere far away. Even though he'd felt anger and resentment towards Mrs. Datta, he'd never wished her any harm. He had always conducted himself with respect in her presence. He knew his place. He couldn't understand why she was so angry with him. After all, he was only doing his job, protecting Mata ji's property, her valuables. She'd humiliated him out in the open, for whatever reason. Maybe she'd done it to put him in his place for being a poor servant. Flustered, Ramu opened the gate and tried to clear his head. With Jawali out on a visit, it was his duty to look after the bungalow. *If she'd been at home,* he thought, *none of this would've happened, and Mrs. Datta wouldn't have dared pull my ear.*

Ramu led Naj into the house and showed him where everything was. Mrs. Datta hurried home, remembering that she'd left dhal on the cooker. Just a few minutes before, Naj had been on the receiving end of Ramu's verbal abuse, but now the tables had turned, the roles had reversed. Naj

Journey Home

was very much the master now and he gave Ramu a serious look. He wanted to get his own back, but that was not his way, so he thought better of it. Ramu was no longer the authoritative figure who had abused him at the gate. He was not even half the man who had stopped him entering his own Grandmother's house. Now, he seemed much smaller, timid and weak. The room fell silent. Ramu was alone with his master and he wasted no time in apologizing again: "I'm sorry about earlier on. I really didn't know who I was dealing with. Mata ji, she never said a word to me about your coming. If she had, sir, I would have greeted you with a garland. That would've been more fitting, sir. When your mother and father come to India, I always greet them with garlands and the children gather around them singing and clapping hands. It's a wonderful scene. And, of course, it makes Mata ji so happy, her happiness is my happiness. She hands out sweets to children, not one or two, they all get a generous handful, and they are not your everyday cheap sweets, but a special variety that comes from Noor Mahal and of course the children love her for that. Mata ji is a much-respected woman and I know my place here but she's like a mother to me and I'd do anything for her. You see, sir, when she's away I'm responsible for everything, everything. That's why I acted the way I did when you turned up at the gate. I'll go and run a shower for you, sir, you'll feel much better after you've cleaned up and I'll have something hot ready waiting for you." Ramu took a step towards the kitchen and it came to him. "You'll need something clean to wear. I'll go and look in your Dad's cupboard. It's full of shirts, trousers and other things. I'm sure I'll find something appropriate for now, and tomorrow I'll take you to the stores and we'll pick up something more in your style."

"Thank you, Ramu."

"No sir, no, please, there is no need for thanks, you see I'm your servant and you are my master. Masters don't thank their servants. It's not the done thing in India, I beg you."

Naj gave him a strange look. He was exhausted and didn't have the energy to argue, but thought Ramu had a remarkably dour personality for a so-called servant. Naj took a much-needed shower. He shaved and dressed in his Dad's old clothes and then ate freshly cooked rice and eggs with salad, washed down with a soft drink. It wasn't Naj's favorite dish but, what the hell, even horse meat would have tasted nice. He hadn't eaten much over the last few days. He felt clean and his belly was full.

Ramu was working in the kitchen when he heard Mrs. Datta's footsteps outside.

"Ramu, where are you?" Mrs. Datta called.

His heart jumped with shock. The terror made him drop a china plate.

"Damn!" said Ramu bitterly, looking at the scattered pieces on the floor. Before he could answer she came into the kitchen.

"Why don't you answer me?" she demanded. "Have you lost your voice?"

Ramu stood shaking nervously, unable to speak, fearing further awful obscenities. She stared at him. His eyes dropped and his legs weakened beneath her gaze.

"Come on, man, speak to me."

"Madam . . . I . . . didn't hear you," he mumbled timidly.

"Why are you wrecking the house in auntie's absence? Have you gone mad?"

"Madam, the saucer just slipped out of my hands. It was an accident," he protested.

"You stupid boy." She was enjoying the fierce thrill of power over him, not for the first time. Ramu bent over and began picking up the broken bits frantically.

Naj heard voices and walked into the kitchen. Mrs. Datta's jaw dropped. She was taken aback by his appearance, she hardly recognized him. *What a transformation, he's so handsome,* she thought.

"Ah, There you are, Naj beta," she said, smiling. Ramu was grateful for his presence.

"Auntie ji. How nice to see you again."

They went through to the living room whilst Ramu released his anger on the laundry basket, kicking it from one side of the kitchen to the other. They sat down on the sofa facing each other.

"Well, I just came by to see you were being cared for," she smiled.

"Everything is fine, Auntie ji. Ramu has been looking after me," he said softly.

Ramu gathered his resolve and came in with two glasses of water for them. "Would you like anything else? Tea, coffee?" he asked.

Naj looked at Mrs. Datta. She shook her head.

"No. That's all," said Naj.

Mrs. Datta lifted her glass and took a deep swallow. "I'm glad you came. Auntie ji will be so thrilled."

Naj yawned suddenly, mouth open, and arms stretched above his head.

"I don't mean to be rude, Auntie ji, but could we have this chat tomorrow? I'm really tired. I must get some sleep."

"Yes, of course." She smiled an embarrassed but gentle smile and stood up. "I have things to do also. I'll drop by later, beta." She moved to the door. "Ramu," she called. He came in hurriedly. "You make sure he gets everything he needs, or you'll have Auntie ji to deal with."

Her demeaning comments were hurtful and more than Ramu could bear. *Maybe, one day, I hope,* he thought, *the stupid cow will come to her senses and be a bit more respectful. On the other hand, like they say: what goes around comes around.*

Naj was relaxed and drowsy. It wasn't long before he dropped off to sleep. It was almost five hours before he woke, his eyes bleary and bloodshot, his whole body perspiring. He wiped the sweat from his forehead and wondered where he was for a second. He had the bewildering sense of being somewhere strange, other than his Grandmother's bungalow, and then it came to him. The light streamed in the open window and made unusual patterns on the floor. He heard Ramu working in the garden. There was the sound of a car horn in the distance and he heard a dog barking close by. He listened to the traffic and voices of children arguing and chattering. He wanted to look outside, but he lay across the bed, arms folded behind his head. He took a deep breath and looked at the ceiling. He couldn't believe what he was seeing. Naj jumped up. "Shit!" he said and shouted for Ramu, who came running into the room, fearing the worst. "What the hell is *that*?" he said nervously, pointing at the ceiling.

"Where, sir?" asked Ramu.

"There, there, up there by the fan."

Ramu recognised it instantly and couldn't help but laugh. "Oh that, that's nothing, sir, it's only a lizard," he said reassuringly. "You'll see them crawling about from time to time, mostly on the ceiling or on the wall, behind the picture frames, nothing to worry about, sir, they are harmless."

"Are you sure they're harmless?"

"Yes sir, quite sure. Let me show you, sir, wait." Ramu rushed outside, lifted a brick and came back with a baby lizard in his hand. "Sir, look, they don't bite, they're totally harmless, and they are more scared of us than we of them." He moved closer and held out his hand. "Sir, you want to hold it?"

"No . . . Take the damn reptile away from me, they give me the creeps."

"Sir, are you scared of them?"

"No. Me, scared? You must be joking. Do you see me shaking? I just don't like them at all. I don't mind dogs and things, but I hate the sight of creepy crawlies."

Ramu burst out laughing but quickly put his hands over his mouth, not wanting to get into further trouble with his master.

"What time is my Grandmother due back?"

"Sir, not long. I bet she's on her way now. She'll be here in an hour or two. I almost phoned her with the news, but thought against it. It'll be a nice surprise for her. She'll be so happy to see you, I know I was. I mean, I am very happy now that you are here, sir."

"How is the old dear?"

"Sir, she's fine, she is very healthy for her age. That's what a lot of people say when they talk about Mata ji. It surprises a lot of people when they find out her real age; she is over ninety, sir."

"Over ninety. I didn't know that. I knew she was old, but over ninety? That is old, really old."

"Sir, she has always looked after herself. She keeps herself active and eats the right kind of food, no meat, no, she doesn't touch meat."

No meat? How can someone survive and stay healthy for ninety years without eating meat? Meat provides essential iron and properties and stuff, Naj thought.

"Sir, no meat, just fresh fruits, vegetables and lots of dhals, sag and traditional roti, either makki or kanak. We don't buy any of that stuff from the market; it's all grown with fertilizers and chemicals. We don't need to, sir, because we grow everything here in the garden. All our vegetables are grown organically come out and see for yourself, sir. Mata ji also routinely takes her walk across the garden, once, twice, three times daily and the cat is a source of company for her. The exercise keeps her fit and healthy."

A knock at the half-open door interrupted their conversation. It was Mrs. Datta.

"Hello, Naj beta, it's me, Mrs. Datta. I just thought I'd come and say a proper hello. I wasn't sure whether you'd be up or not." She was all dressed up in a sari, wearing black leather shoes and with light make-up on her face. "I did try knocking on the front door but I don't think you heard me," she said apologetically.

"Hello Auntie ji, good to see you again. Please make yourself at home in the living room. I'll be out in a minute," Naj said. "Ramu," he continued. "Go and attend to Auntie ji' needs and I'll join her in a few minutes." The unscheduled meeting had thrown Naj and he wondered if it was common practice in India for a neighbor to drop in unannounced.

"Yes, sir," said Ramu, doubtfully. He felt uncomfortable about facing Mrs. Datta so soon after his humiliation in front of his new master, but he had no choice. He knew his place; he was a servant and that was that, he had to obey the commands of his masters. Nothing less, nothing more. He rolled his eyes and went to attend to Mrs. Datta, whilst Naj went to the washroom.

Bonita, Mrs. Datta's daughter, tapped frantically on the door and Ramu rushed out to see who it was.

"Hello Bonita, what's wrong? You look as though you've seen a ghost."

"Yes, no, I mean, is my mother here?"

"I'm here, beta, what's the matter?" Her voice came towards them from the passage.

"Mata ji, come." She pointed to her bedroom, her body shaking, lips trembling, her heart throbbing like a wound. Mrs. Datta knew instantly what the problem was. She understood what Bonita was saying.

"Calm down, beta, calm down."

"Come on, mother, hurry up!" Her eyes were burning. Both of them hurried back to their house.

I don't know what is the matter with this girl, scared by a little teeny weeny spider. How is she going to cope with life once I'm gone? She'll be a laughing stock if she behaves like this at her in-laws' house. Mrs. Datta shook her head in frustration.

"Kamlee, kamlee, kamlee," Mrs. Datta muttered as she swung past Bonita and inside. Poor Bonita had a phobia about insects, and her mother had failed to support her to overcome such fears. Instead, she put them down to her daughter being a weak person. Each time it happened she got nothing but complaints from her mother.

I can't understand my mother, Bonita thought. *She always goes into a mood. Why? She knows what I'm like when I see a daddy-long-legs, spiders, lizards and other things. I'm studying at college level and have always achieved top grades, I'm bright and sensible, so what makes me a kamlee?* Rubbing her earlobe thoughtfully, Bonita followed her mother into the house.

Ramu felt more at ease with Mrs. Datta out of the way. He whistled about the garden without a care and attended to his plants. He had always felt happier with them than with people. They didn't talk back or put him down like Mrs. Datta did. He thought she was an awful pain in the ass.

Naj came to the living room hoping to find Mrs. Datta. There was no one there except a cat sleeping on the sofa.

"Ramu," Naj called, "where are you?" He walked out and met Ramu by the front door.

"You called, sir?"

"Yes, where's that lady, what's-her-name from next door?"

"She's not here, sir."

"I can see that, but where is she?"

"She's gone home, sir."

"Oh well." Naj shrugged. "I am sure she'll turn up unannounced again."

"Can I make you something to drink or eat, sir?"

"Not just yet, Ramu. Just show me the way to the kitchen and I'll make a cup of coffee myself. I take it we have coffee in the house."

"Yes, sir, let me show you where everything is, sir."

With a cup of coffee in his hand, Naj shuffled around the house, going from room to room. The family room was large and spacious. There were two long bulky sofas that could accommodate many bottoms, a large wooden coffee table and peacock feathers in a bronze pot. Looking up, he found himself face-to-face with a group of photos on the wall, old black-and-white ones. The faces were familiar to him. The woman looked like a younger Grandmother

Journey Home

and the boy looked like his Dad. The man with a beard and turban who towered over them must be his Granddad. He found the photo fascinating. He stood rooted, looking at it for ages. Then he stared at another picture. It was a photograph of himself. The little boy who stared out at him was himself, Naj Dulak. He was moved, and couldn't help but smile thinking about the days gone by. He looked again, and laughed about his hair style. There was an old rocking chair, the seat covered with handmade Mogul-designed cloth. Shaanti, Jawali's cat, slept there except when it was occupied by her. He could smell the freshness of furniture polish. A smell of spicy cooking wafted in from the kitchen. Naj walked into his Grandmother's bedroom. Sure enough, the walls were plastered with Karina Kapoor's photographs, as his mother had told him. He was amused. Outside the one-storey bungalow was a well-maintained garden with a vegetable patch, flower beds, and banana trees that stood majestically alongside the dense sugarcane bush and the papaya tree. The place was surrounded by a five foot wall. There were two gates, one to the front and the other at the rear, both padlocked and rarely used. There was a table and some chairs in the patio area. With the blue sky above and the sound of the mynah bird singing from a mango tree by the roadside, it was a picture of paradise. The whole area seemed as if magic had been at work in its creation. The spacious, pink bungalow was everything he had hoped it would be. In fact, it had turned out to be much more beautiful. He was fascinated with everything; smells, colours, the bungalow's location. "Ah yes," he breathed, the garden had a sweet smell.

Ramu had been at work, tending to his chores without a word of complaint. He took pride in all his tasks and knew his place in the presence of his employers. He was a servant.

Naj sipped his coffee and slowly moved around the garden, relishing the merry gold carnations, violets and roses and admiring Ramu's hard work. Flowers bloomed in the early morning sun and perfumed the air. A bee hummed by, spinning in and out over the beds in search of flowers to creep inside. The scent of the flowers was intoxicating. He enjoyed the warmth of the sun under the shade of a banana tree and glanced at his watch. It was almost five-thirty. *Grandmother should be here very soon*, he thought. He kept glancing towards the road for signs of her car. He was excited about seeing his Grandmother in the flesh and his heart raced faster by the minute. For a moment he was lost in this new world full of strange sights, sounds, smells and customs. It was a madhouse of human upheaval and confusion. Here, no one was physically restrained; the yelling, shouting, pushing, shoving, hugging, spitting and eyeballing were everyday things.

Naj looked at his watch again. It was now six-thirty p.m. and he wondered how he was going to greet her and what he was going to say to her, when the sound of an engine suddenly interrupted his reverie. A car drew up outside the house, the door swung open and an elderly woman emerged. She was small and slim with straight silvery hair tied into a bun at the back of her head and a shawl across her shoulders. She held her walking stick and glanced towards the house with excitement. She held her breath for a second and, to her surprise, felt a shiver run down to her spine. Every time Darsh came back from England she felt like this.

Ramu ran to give her the news about Naj's arrival. Before he muttered a word, she somehow knew that he'd arrived.

Journey Home

"He's here, Mata ji . . . he's here," said Ramu excitedly.

"I know, I can smell him from here. Now," she demanded, "bring my things into the house."

"Yes, Mata ji."

She walked through the gate. There, by the front door, a tall, slim figure with a lightly tanned, face started to walk towards her. He radiated an intense, warm smile and she instantly knew that he was her own flesh and blood. They met by the gate and hugged, their arms wrapped around each other. Naj could see tears glistening in her eyes. This was a special moment for both of them. It felt good, really good. She had been waiting for this moment for years.

"Let me look at you," she said, gazing into his eyes. Her hands trembled with excitement. She smiled. "You have your Dad's eyes and nose." They hugged again. When Naj spoke, his eyes rested fondly on her, and they walked up the garden path together, arms linked as he listened attentively to her. She noticed that he had broad shoulders and a strong bone structure. She was overwhelmed by her first impressions of him.

To Naj, his Grandmother looked older than he had expected. She was ancient, though no one really knew exactly how old Jawali Dulak was. She was older than anyone else he knew, even older than the Queen of England. She talked of things that others had heard only at second hand. As far as anyone knew, old Mata ji Jawali had been around forever, longer than anyone could remember. Newborns themselves had become parents and recalled the same kind old face and perpetually graying head of hair that was always neatly tied into a knot. To them she was unchanging, ageless, even her taste in clothes remained traditional and simple. The community leaders and neighbors had all acquired old Mata ji's wisdom. She was a prominent figure within the community. Everyone behaved respectfully in her presence, taking care not to speak out of turn. She always replied in the same quiet, measured tone that reassured, putting others at ease. She needed no extraordinary qualifications to affirm her standing, her very presence was enough to sort out local disputes, feuds and quarrels. She was unique, one of a kind. This was the first time in his life that Naj had been that close to such an old person. It didn't feel strange at all—the opposite, in fact. It felt warm and wonderful. He thought very highly of her; she was confident, kind, dignified; simply an intriguing woman. She reminded him of Mother Teresa of Kolkata.

Jawali lived on the outskirts of the city in the suburb of Cantonment. The locals called it "Cantt " for short. It was a mixture of bungalows and houses set in a crescent on a street named Rastoorba Nagar. Cantonment was an Army base developed by the British during their colonial rule. In 1947, the British had left and the Indian government continued its administration. The army recruits in their green combat uniforms were often seen engaging in military exercises, marching up and down on the Mehsampur Road, stomping their feet. The area of Shawnee had both an army and civilian population. It had its own sabjee mandi where everyday the locals purchased anything from okra, tinda and white parsnips to kashmiri mirch harvested fresh from the local farms. There were many other shops in the main square, some specializing in the latest trends and fashions, from shoes, clothing, electrical goods, hair styling, desi sweet shops, food takeaways and general food stores. There were video and DVD rentals, shoe menders, doctors and animal feed stores. One could purchase almost anything and everything. Naj's first impression of the

Journey Home

neighborhood was that everything in it was larger than life. It was overwhelming.

Back in the house, a candle burned brightly on a small table. The soft sound of the religious hymns being aired on the radio, had a soothing effect on the cat and her owner. It was comfortable and homely. That evening after supper Jawali sat on the side of his bed and the two of them talked. She told him she was proud to be Indian. She liked the Indian way of life, its traditions, customs and religion. She liked its colors, the seasons, and everything connected to the past. It was almost midnight before Naj finally went off to sleep. Jawali was tired and sleepy too, but couldn't resist watching him sleep peacefully; her beautiful, tall, handsome, educated grandson. She knew there might not be many opportunities like this and she wanted to enjoy every second with him; every second was precious. After all, she was almost ninety years of age, so for her this was pure magic. She had been waiting for such a moment for a very long time. She had often asked Darsh for Naj to be sent over so that they could get to know each other, spend time together. She had so much to share with him and many things to teach. She felt that he was missing out on many important things about the Eastern way of life; the cultural and religious knowledge, the extended family system, the respect for elders. She was angry with his father, even though Darsh was her only child. *I will have words with him, I will tell him.* The voice in her head shook with fury. She had come close to hating him for denying her the opportunity of seeing Naj growing up. Naj too had missed out on the special bond between grandparent and grandchild because of his irresponsible parents. Rising, she leaned over with tears of happiness in her eyes, gently kissed him on the forehead and whispered, "Sweet dreams, mere putter." She switched off the lamp, and slowly walked out of the room. *I'm so pleased he's finally here,* she thought. *My heart isn't aching anymore.* Outside, the sky was star-studded and graced with a silvery moon. She watched the universe in its splendor, an endless cavalcade of twinkling stars.

"Just imagine, I'm standing outside under the moonlight in the warm March air. If every night was like tonight, it would be wonderful," she muttered. "It would've been tragically sad for us both if something had happened to me before we had a chance to meet. I will treasure every moment with him while he's here."

Next morning, at the stroke of seven, she walked into his room and woke him up. "Naj, it's time to get up," she called softly, leaning over him.

"Who is it?"

"It's me, Grandmother. I'm here, my darling. I'm here. Rise and shine, putter."

He managed to open one eye and ask what time it was.

"It's time you were up. It's gone seven, dear."

"Seven? That's much too early, Grandma," Naj replied as he turned over and closed his eyes again.

"You need to rise, beta, we are going to the temple this morning."

"Why, what for?"

"Don't ask silly questions." Her eyes were earnestly fixed on him.

"It would help if I knew exactly why you were planning to take me to the gurdwara," he pressed.

"OK, baba, since you've asked, I'm taking you there for a dose of spiritual healing and tomorrow we'll go to masjid first and then to the temple." It was the truth, as far as it went. "Don't you go to the house of God in England?"

"No, Grandma, I don't and neither do Mum and Dad."

"Why not?" she asked abruptly.

"I just don't, Grandma." *The only temple I go to is the Hare and Hounds, my local pub,* he thought.

"Well, OK. You are going to the temple this morning and I'm the one who'll be taking you there and that's final," she said firmly.

Oh dear, he thought. He listened silently as she continued: "I go to the temple almost every day. It's very important for us to pay respects to our creator. You know he is the reason for us all being here on this earth; we owe everything to him, our minds, bodies, and souls." She moved to the window and drew the curtains. The sun lit up the room and he hid his face under the covers. She touched him lightly. "Now, religion," she paused. "Are you listening? Religion is a way of life for us in the East," she said with pride and confidence. "It's the basis of family and of a strong nation." He removed the covers from his face and looked at her. Now he noticed a few more wrinkles on her face and more of her dentures glittering white.

Naj still looked tired to her, but his smile was infectious. She brushed her hair back with her hand and quickly changed the subject: "You know, beta, young people, they seem to care more for the latest trends and fashions than for their faith these days. I can't understand it."

"If you say so, Grandma." *So far as she's concerned*, he thought, *it's the truth*.

"It's those damn Bollywood films. They're ruining our society and way of life; ruining the moral fiber of our nation." She put a hand into her side pocket and pulled out a small handful of almonds. "Hold out your hand, beta." She put four almonds into his hand and one into her own mouth and began chewing. "Almonds are very good for your health; your Granddad, bless him, ate four almonds every day and he was much healthier for it. He'd have liked a bowlful each day, but that's all we could afford at the time." She sat down and cleared her throat. "Don't you like them?" she pressed.

"I'll have them later, Grandmother." He didn't like nuts at all, full stop, unless they were coated with thick chocolate, but he didn't wish to hurt her feelings.

"Yes, good, you make sure they are part of your everyday diet."

Suddenly she went quiet. "Ah, yes," she continued. "As I was saying before, it's greed, that's all it is. It's all about making as much money as possible from anything and everything as far as those greedy film makers are concerned." She stood up and straightened herself with the aid of her walking stick. A strange sound came from her mouth, the kind of sound one hears when a prey has been pierced through the heart with a hunter's arrow. "We are a doomed race; mark my words."

"Why is that, Grandmother?"

"Because we are chained to the West, especially to America. It's a sinking ship, and we all know it. Everyone over here is trying to live the American dream; big homes, cars and everything else that goes with it. This is India, for God's sake; we have millions and millions of mouths to feed. America is not our role model, its values and life styles are not good for our race, culture, country or religions. We have enough problems in-house to deal with. For instance, thousands of Biharis have poured into Panjab, and they are still arriving in bus loads every single day. Nobody's doing anything about it. I don't mind them coming over to work, but they come with their filthy lifestyle of drug-pushing, drug-abuse, encouraging our vulnerable young men and destroying families as a direct result."

Naj was surprised by his Grandmother's knowledge of different topics and her ability to change the subject and return to it later without any difficulty. *There is nothing wrong with her mind, memory, or spirit,* he thought. *She's as sharp as the next person. That's amazing for someone of ninety or more.*

"I have complained to our local politician Mr. Bhatty," she continued. "He didn't help. All he said was: 'The public demands those kinds of films, it's good for the Indian economy, and they generate millions of rupees from all over the world.' I told him money wasn't everything and he seemed to agree with me on that point." She sat down again. "If I had my way, I would ban all those filthy films where half-naked girls are seen revealing their breasts and backsides. It's disgusting and vulgar. It's not Indian, that is my view, but who listens to me? As for those Biharis, I would send them all back to Bihar." She frowned and continued, "They say I'm living in the past, how wrong can one be?" She leaned towards his head and tugged at his covers. "Are you listening to me?"

He pulled a face like a tortoise sticking its head out of its shell. "Yes, Grandmother, I have heard every word that came from your mouth."

"So what do think, putter?"

Naj sat up and looked at her. "You mustn't demand too much from politicians and film makers. Society has changed a lot since your day. It's different now. People want much more these days. You know what?"

"What?"

"Well, nothing stands still; everything has to move forward. It's always been that way, in the past things moved at a slower pace, but now with new technical advances everything moves that much faster."

"I'm sure you're right, but . . . in the old days they made films that were entertaining with a good story line, about real lives and real people." She looked at the clock, it was almost nine. "Naj beta, jaldi say oothoe na, [hurry up and rise]. It's almost mid-day. What do you want for breakfast? How about scrambled eggs with paraothas and yogurt, your favorite?" she shuffled out of the room.

"All right, I'll be up in a minute." He didn't feel much like breakfast, but thought he must make an effort for her sake. If he told her she'd be on his case all day about not eating, about food, about those poor people who had to survive on rats and stuff because they couldn't afford to buy everyday food. Not that he minded her moaning, but sometimes she went over the top, on and on. She had a habit of complaining if things were not to her liking. She moaned unnecessarily about things that did not concern her. He loved her, absolutely, he loved her to bits. It felt good to be with her. He wondered how he had managed so far without her going on at him. He knew she would not let it go unless he got out of bed and into the washroom. She put her head around the door and looked at him with an appraising, critical eye. There was no getting away from it; this was her domain.

"Ah," she said, "You'd better hurry up and get washed. Ramu has prepared our breakfast." It was clear from her expression that she wasn't very impressed with him.

Naj wasn't religious. He could not remember Mum and Dad ever taking him to any place of worship. Although he had been to the village church with the school on two occasions he didn't experience any special form of spiritual healing there. However, he felt duty-bound. Besides, how could he say no to her? After all, she was his Grandmother. He sat up slowly, looking at his watch. It was quarter past midnight.

That's wrong, it can't be, he thought. Then it came to him that he had forgotten to adjust his watch to the Indian time. Outside the sun was rising and the world was buzzing with activity. Children were on their way to school on rickshaws and autos. Ramu was working away at the vegetable patch, digging, weeding and watering, while the sweat poured off his back and the flies played hide-and-seek around his head. The postman delivered letters and parcels. The sabjee man shouted for trade at the top of his lungs. A big, burly, holy man stood silently outside the iron gate, his face covered with dirt and chapatti flour, several beaded chains hanging around his neck and a bag hanging from his shoulder. He held a long stick in his hand as he waited for God-given offerings of food or money, although he preferred cash. Even the sacred cow was out strolling in the street for breakfast, chewing up bits of paper, cardboard or any old rubbish she could find. People had been up at the break of the day, some as early as four or five o'clock. The morning prayers echoed around the neighborhood. It was all part of everyday life and nothing like England where some people stayed in bed until lunch-time. *But that's not the done thing here,* Naj thought. *Everyone has to do their bit for family, community and country.*

Naj shaved and showered quickly and headed for the veranda. Jawali beckoned him to a seat next to her at the table, where they could have breakfast without being disturbed.

"This is nice, Grandmother. It's paradise," he said, looking around.

"Ramu, come on beta, nashta (breakfast)."

"Yes, Mata ji."

"I'm so pleased you like it. The lord has been very kind, this is all his creation, you included." She dabbed her eyes with a wisp of creamy embroidered handkerchief.

"Has he?"

She rested her hand on his knee. "He truly has," she said. "I'm so grateful to Baba ji for sending my lovely grandson to me after all this time."

Naj looked into her eyes and could tell she meant every word. He leaned across and hugged her.

"Thank you beta, I'm so glad you did that, I have been longing for your hugs and kisses for a long, long time," said Jawali, feeling very emotional and happy. "Now, we have a lot of catching up to do. First, tell me about your life back in England and then I need to know your future plans."

Naj's thoughts drifted back to Hertfordshire as soon as the word "England" left her mouth. His eyes fixed on two mynah birds grooming one another up a tree. They reminded him of Lucy, his girlfriend. When they first met, Naj wasn't looking for love or a long-term relationship. All he was interested in was a bit of fun at a party. They got talking and both had a little too much to drink. Before they realized what was happening they found themselves attracted to each other and Lucy became the queen of his heart. Naj smiled, the love and longing on his face pleasing Jawali, who was surprised by his unexpected manliness.

"Yes beta, do talk, I want to know everything, and I mean *everything*" cried Jawali, with a mixture of defiance and despair in her face that startled Naj.

"Breakfast is ready, Mata ji," said Ramu. "Would you like me to serve now?"

"Yes beta, lay aaho [do serve]."

Ramu moved swiftly with the prepared food and placed it on the table, his eyes on Naj as he served. He envied him. His eyes were travelling from his head to his toes. He was everything Ramu wished he was, tall, handsome, light-skinned and wealthy. Suddenly, Ramu felt sick thinking about his own situation. *I am nothing but a reject,* the words in his mind mocked. *I don't want to be a servant all my life. I will change my status one day even if it kills me.* A kind of nausea overtook him and momentarily his head swam. He asked more questions of himself: *What are you doing here, Ramu?*

Jawali and Naj continued to talk as they ate paraothas with fresh yogurt made from buffalo milk, mango pickle, scrambled eggs and lassi. He'd had paraothas in England before but couldn't remember them being as tasty.

"I used to make paraothas all by myself, at the age of eight, for the whole family," Jawali said, apologetically. "My limbs as they are now won't let me make paraothas I get of pain in my hands, especially this right one so it's impossible, but I do miss making paraothas."

Ramu put down two plates of food.

"It's a special skill," Jawali continued. "Not everyone can make tasty paraothas. It takes a lifetime to master such skills. My father used to tell me that my cooking was the best in the whole village. He loved my cooking better than my mother's or anyone else in our family. I loved cooking for him, so at the age of ten I completely took over the family's kitchen, I wouldn't allow anyone else in there." She looked up; he was taking a keen interest in her story. He caught glimpses of her expression as she talked, her voice clear.

It was a bright warm morning. The garden was gay with color, and the warm air wafted the scent of flowers to them.

For a moment they stared at each other, her face lit by the sunlight. He sat across the table and studied her. Her skin was soft, her eyes misty and beautiful.

Jawali resumed her conversation: "We didn't have many pots and pans but what we had were useful and I made sure that they were kept clean at all times. Back then our situation was no different to others in the village. Times were hard and people shared everything with each other. We all borrowed things from each other and returned them whenever we could. We always did; there was this trust among people. Everyone was in the same boat except for the money-lender. He was the scum of the earth, he really was." The money-lender stirred her emotions and transported her back to the past. Her body stiffened and her expression sharpened. "Let me tell you, one year the rain failed to come and the crops were very poor. The price of wheat rocketed and families struggled to feed themselves. My father had no choice that year but to ask for a loan."

Naj looked at her. "Grandmother, tell me more about your teenage years."

"Ah," she laughed. "What? You mean when I was young."

"Yes, Mata ji."

"OK." She adjusted her posture and began: "We were never young, no, it wasn't allowed back then, either you were a child or you were a grown-up, there was no in-between in those days, no time for teenage years as you put it. As far as everyone was concerned, I was an adult as soon as I was able to cook and clean. I think I was about seven or eight years old when I started taking over from mother. It was normal, you were expected to help out, no question about it."

"You were doing all that at the age of seven?"

"Yes, it's true. All my sahelis [girl friends] were in the same boat as me."

"I'm shocked, to say the least. So . . . you mean to tell me you never had time to play?"

"We played, of course we played. When the work was finished we all got together and played in the village square, usually before the sun went down. Don't get me wrong; we had lots of time for fun and games. I used to make my own guddian and patolay from bits of old clothing and wool. It was magic. You see, we girls never went to school in those days, we were not allowed and never studied. That's why I can't read or write, but hey, I'm as smart as the next person. All my knowledge and skills came from my elders, especially my mother, who taught me everything I needed for the journey ahead as a woman," said Jawali. After a pause, she added, "Whenever we had relatives or visitors around, my mother asked me to prepare food for them. Everyone used to tell me what a great cook I was and that God had given me this great gift. Of course, those compliments were music to my ears. I used to be so happy. I was married to your granddad at the young age of twelve, a mere child by today's standards. But in those days I was considered to be a woman of marriageable age. I was engaged to my husband at the age of five."

Naj found this funny. He began to laugh: "You're kidding me, Grandmother."

With her eyebrows knitted, she looked straight at him: "You laugh all you want, mere beta, but it's true; that is how things were back then. Children had no say in the matter. You went along with your parents' wishes, no one dared to ask questions. Their decision was final, like it or not. Respect and honor were paramount and still apply in Indian culture today. Family elders determined what was right and what was wrong. They always had their children's interest at heart. I have never known a parent who wished to do anything bad towards their own child or harm them in any way. It was not the done thing by ninety-nine percent of parents, but I can tell you stories about the remaining one percent who sinned in order to protect the honor of their family or closest relatives. A person would go to any lengths. Bringing shame on one's family or dishonoring them in any way was always dealt with seriously. The consequences were harsh. I know of many stories of honor killings where girls vanished from the family home and were never seen again, because they happened to fall in love with a boy their family did not approve of. There are many such true stories: just ask people in any of the villages in Panjab, Uttar Pradesh, Haryana, or other villages throughout India, Pakistan, and Bangladesh. This sort of thing is still prevalent today. I've heard that, every six hours, somewhere in India a young woman is beaten to death or driven to commit suicide. Of course, it used to be much worse, but society has moved on since and the young people of today have a lot more say in the matter of marriage. However, family honor is paramount to all respectable families in the Eastern culture. I trust you are taking note of what I'm saying. Family honor is the cornerstone of our culture. Everyone has to abide by the cultural norms and traditions. Those who break away lose all respect from the family and the community."

"This . . . honor thing, it sounds very dangerous to me, Grandmother."

Jawali glanced at Naj, and could see he was absorbed in her story. "One has to stay within the boundaries, beta. If they are crossed, one could end up mutilated, burnt alive, or beaten to death."

"Really?" Naj was horrified.

Journey Home

"Yes." Jawali nodded vigorously.

"That sounds very harsh, especially at an age when you need to experiment with things. I understand the meaning of respect and abide by it, but this family honor thing I'm not at all sure of."

She knew what she was talking about, he understood what she meant, about life, respect, culture, traditions and values. Although she had never learned to read or write, she had a great gift of learning and storing knowledge of all kinds from everyday experience. Ninety years of knowledge and more, together with a perfect memory, is very rare. Even now, she could be asked about anything from living off the land to the Mogul Empire and she would answer in detail.

"Grandmother," Naj asked, "can I ask you a question that has bothered me since I arrived?"

"What is it, beta?"

"Its people, I mean there are masses of people everywhere I look, why?"

"What do you mean 'why'?" Jawali looked at him in confusion.

"I mean, where have they all come from?"

"What do you mean 'where have they come from'? They are all home-produced, they are all Indians, of course. Don't you have people in England?"

"Yes, but not this many."

"Well, then England is a very small country, isn't it?"

"Yes, but . . ."

"Let me tell you about India and its people. India is huge and has many religions, traditions, and belief systems. Indian society believes in large families and that every child born is a gift from God." Her plain cotton dupatta [scarf] fell to the ground from her bony shoulders as she leaned forward. Before she realized it, Naj bent over and picked it up. "Ah, thank you, beta. You see, in India the child mortality rate is exceptionally high, especially amongst the poor, and that's another reason for having a large number of children."

Naj felt more confused than ever before and wanted more clarification about the Indian way of life. "I see," he said, moving forward in his seat. "Can you explain a bit more about child mortality?"

"Of course," she folded her hands front of her as Naj broke another piece off the paraotha and dipped it into the yogurt pot before putting it into his mouth. "People here are very superstitious, and they have many false beliefs and compulsions. Young mothers and their families are driven by superstitions and wrong beliefs, such as breastfeeding only after seeing a star or a moon, or that a mother cannot breastfeed a baby until at least three days after birth."

Ramu approached the table: "Do you require anything, Mata ji?" She waved him away without making eye contact.

Naj asked another question that had been on his mind: "Why didn't you move to England with Mum and Dad?"

"Foreign ways do not agree with me, beta. I would never be happy in England. For one, it's too cold for my liking and for another I'd never pick up the language. I'd be bored to death. Besides, this bungalow is my home, a home with feelings. It's comfortable and I have everything I need here except for my children."

Naj admired her honesty. She was very much her own woman.

At about half past nine they walked quietly to the temple. Naj did not speak. His Grandmother tried to make conversation on several occasions during the journey that took about ten minutes. Faces passing turned to stare and he gave them a mildly offended look. His mind was occupied with a great loss. A great loss indeed. He had lost a great friend, he grieved. Sonia's death weighed heavily on him. It had been a bitter blow, losing her like that. He wanted to do something for her and did not know what would be appropriate. He observed everything that came before him. When they were half way, they were approached by two little girls of about ten in tattered clothes with messy, dirty hair, pleading eyes and grubby hands thrust forward: "God bless your family; God will give you a beautiful, healthy son so please give generously to us poor souls."

At first Naj was captivated by their presence. Then he looked at them as they continued to harass him by tugging at his shirt. Now he looked at them with distaste and wasn't sure what to do. The girls were defiant and determined to get money; they were insistent.

Jawali looked at the girls with a critical eye. "Ignore them, putter," she said and plodded on. By now Naj's patience was tested to the maximum. He quickened his pace in order to leave the beggar girls behind. It seemed that the girls were on a mission. In the end their tactics proved successful, and Naj grudgingly handed over a 10 rupee note.

The temple rose in front of them, a place where God lived and had an answer to his problem. He followed her without a word like a newly-born calf following its mother, walking with his head down, two steps behind her. No one noticed their arrival. Jawali took off her shoes, washed her hands at the tap, and entered, ringing a bell. She raised her hands before her face and sat on the hard floor beside other worshippers listening to a recital of hymns from the Geeta. New worshipers came in, paid their respects, took parsad and left. Jawali lit a candle and Naj followed her. He watched her praying with her hand to her face, then sat down and enjoyed the Geeta. He had never before paid much attention to the house of God but felt the compelling need to say a prayer for Sonia. There were half-a-dozen other worshipers in the hall, meditating, making wishes, making offerings, receiving parsad and saying prayers. Naj felt traumatized and, as he was in God's house, it suddenly came to him. He stood up, folded his hands, said a heart-felt prayer and asked God for the salvation of her soul. He also made offerings in her name and a small financial donation to the temple's funds. He felt soothed, the weight lifted from his shoulders. He also felt blessed for some strange reason, sensing the tension and anger leave his body. The process of being healed lifted his mood and his thoughts turned to Sonia once more. She had been kind, considerate, and beautiful. She had been his friend by chance, by accident, by fate. They had similar interests, and she was quite different from anyone he knew; she made him feel good about himself. He related to her and the two of them had shared brief but happy moments. She had left a lasting impression on him. The impact of losing her so suddenly had had a greater impact on his well-being than not playing football for England at Wembley. Sonia had died tragically, so young. She had had her whole life before her. They had exchanged phone numbers and planned to meet in Jalandhar the following week. He didn't want to let her go, but let her go he had to, a young woman who had been so beautiful, fresh and outgoing, and with whom he had instantly bonded.

*

Journey Home

Jawali's sharp eye and maternal heart sensed that all was not well with her grandson. He looked emotionally drained and weak. She noticed his long silences and expressionless face as he mopped around the house. She worried about this and began to lose sleep, wondering what could be bothering him. She had spoken to his Mum and Dad on the phone about his low mood and they had no idea why Naj had suddenly become withdrawn. Maybe it was the food or the weather, they thought. Darsh had also spoken to him about it and Naj had assured his Dad that they had nothing to be concerned about. He found his Grandmother over-sensitive at times and had noticed she worried over little things needlessly. After all, she was ninety and that had to influence the way she saw situations. Naj tried hard to be cheerful and carefree in her presence so that she was no wiser about his problems, but the old lady asked him question after question and he felt he couldn't bottle it up any longer. Later that day, they were having afternoon tea on the veranda. She chose this moment to put it to him.

"What's wrong, why are you so quiet? Is something bothering you?" She paused and looked at him. "You know you can trust your Grandmother."

"I'm just tired, Grandmother, just tired" said Naj. But she was sure there was something serious behind his low mood that bothered him.

"I'm going to rest, if you don't mind."

"No, of course not, why should I mind? I'm little tired myself. You go and rest, beta. I'll tell Ramu to bring your roti in there when you're ready to eat."

For years, Jawali had liked to have a brief snooze in the afternoon. It didn't matter whether she was seated in her rocking chair or lying down on the sofa, she'd get almost unbearably sleepy and within seconds she'd be snoozing with her mouth open wide. With the passing of time her snoozes had become longer and longer. Sometimes she'd be sitting there, eyes shut tight and it was hard to tell whether she was just resting or snoozing. Ramu had his own theory.

Naj let out a long breath. *I wish Sonia hadn't died like that,* he thought. *I wish I could tell Lucy or Tom or somebody close to get it off my chest. On the other hand, I don't want them be worried unnecessarily. There's no point telling Mum and Dad for the same reason. I can't tell Grandmother, although she is quick, thoughtful and caring. She's too old and vulnerable, and I can't take that chance with her. I don't want to alarm any of them. It would be much simpler just to keep quiet, it's only for another sixteen days or so and then I'll be back in England. I'll go and see my GP for some counselling or something. The time will pass quickly. Maybe I'll be able to share it with Lucy and Tom."*

Later that evening Ramu had supper of wheat chapattis with sagh and added a dollop of mango pickle for a spicy taste. He poured a glass of lassi to wash it down. Humming a tune from a Bollywood film, he carried the tray to Naj's bedroom. He stood at the door and called, "It's Ramu, sir, your roti."

"Come in." Naj's voice had a strange tone. He was half-asleep lying flat on his bed with the fan spinning at maximum speed, which cooled the air and kept away the mosquitoes. "I'm glad to see you relaxing, sir," he couldn't resist adding. He tried to make eye contact with him but Naj's eyes were shut tight. "I'll leave it on the table, sir. Have it when you feel like it. If you need anything else just give me a holler, sir." He deposited the tray on the table and left the room, closing the door behind him.

The next morning Jawali looked in on Naj and found him fast asleep. She noticed his roti untouched where Ramu

Journey Home

had left it on the table. She frowned. "It's no wonder he's always tired, he doesn't eat his food properly," Jawali said, moving to his bedside. "Naj beta, wake up, you can't sleep on an empty stomach." He slowly opened his eyes and looked at her motherly face. "Today, beta, I'm going to feed you with my own hands and I will enjoy it immensely. Come on, putter, it's time you were up, I'll get Ramu to prepare us a breakfast and I'm going to feed you myself." Ramu was outside tending to the vegetable patch and she shouted at him out the window, "Ramu, go and make some paraothas for two of us, and hurry up."

Naj sat up and leaned against the headboard. "Grandmother, can we talk?"

"Certainly, beta. First brush your teeth and take a shower, and we'll eat and talk at the breakfast table," answered Jawali happily as she turned to him from the window.

Naj needed to tell her what had happened on his journey. He could not keep it bottled up inside. The pain was so great. He couldn't hold it in any longer. But he was a smart and thoughtful young man, and never leaped before checking out all the pitfalls.

"Come and sit down, Grandmother, there is something I would like to share with you, something you should know." An anxious, concerned expression came over her face instantly. She could tell from his tone that it was serious. Something in his face suggested bad news, but she hoped it was something to do with the change of environment or that he was suffering from jetlag.

"What is it, beta? Not bad news, I hope?" she asked, taking a seat at the end of his bed.

"Not there, Mata ji, come and sit next to me." He put his arm over her shoulders, holding her tightly. "I'm sorry," he said, and she knew it was bad news. His voice was emotional but steady. He told her everything from the minute he stepped off the plane, how he met Sonia, the horrific coach accident, and how lucky he was to be alive. She was anxious about the pain he felt. It was a very emotional for them, and they comforted each other as tears were shed.

"Naj beta, why didn't you tell me this before? Keeping it all bottled up inside, something as serious as what you've been through. It almost broke my heart to see you so dreadfully pale. I hope you won't make a habit of keeping secrets from me." She paused because she was feeling faint.

"I didn't mean to, Mata ji, it's just that I was wounded so deeply and felt confused. I never want to live through that experience again."

Although she was bruised and grieved by his every word, Jawali put her arms around him, and gently told him that he was brave, and that she loved him with all her heart. Furthermore, she was very proud of him. Her tone was warm and caring. She always spoke like that to Naj, but when she spoke to Ramu her tone would automatically become more high-pitched, yet still with an element of kindness. If one had to take anything away from an encounter with her, it was her gift of respect and kindness.

Naj thought his Grandmother impeccably wise, elegant, kind and beautiful, more beautiful than anyone in the whole world except his girlfriend, Lucy.

Jawali wiped away a tear as she spoke: "It's fate that you are here now, beta." Her voice was calming. "You and Sonia were sitting together and the Lord took her and not you." She sighed and the room fell silent for several heartbeats before she spoke again. "Baba ji protected you from harm and I am so grateful to the almighty. I'm sad that a young life has been lost amongst many others. I really feel for them and their families, but sometimes it is God's will and we just have to accept it."

"I've lost all your gifts from Mum and Dad. I'm sorry."

"Don't worry about material things. They can be replaced at any time. But a life can't be replaced." Naj suddenly felt like crying. "From what you tell me about her, she was a real diamond, and it would have been a pleasure to meet her." She paused for breath, anguish across her face. "You know what you must do now, beta?"

"What's that, Mata ji?"

"You must contact her parents one way or another, either you arrange to visit them or by any other means, so that you can explain what happened and how. Hearing directly from you may give them some comfort, as you were her friend and were with her when she passed away. If your Granddad was alive he would give you the same advice: Do what you have to, but do it right and you'll feel proud of yourself as well as taking your place among the respected and honorable men of our family."

"Yes, Mata ji, I promise."

Jawali was pleased with his response. She had expected nothing less. "Do your best, and be honest with them."

Naj turned his attention to his inner self and wondered how and when he was going to deal with this great responsibility. Had he the strength to look into Sonia's parents' eyes and tell them the truth, the whole truth and nothing but the truth? He was engulfed in a torment of guilt.

Jawali's eyes were still on him. "Kya baat hai beta [what's wrong]? Why are you so quiet?" she asked.

"Oh, I'm just thinking."

"Thinking?"

"Yes, Grandmother, I'm thinking about what you've just said."

"What is there to think about? It's your duty. Nothing can be worse than losing a child for a parent. I am sure they are devastated with the grief of losing their young, beautiful daughter. You know it's not easy for any parent to come to terms with the loss of a child."

Naj wasn't used to being under so much pressure and felt like a fish out of water.

"Beta, you have to promise me that you'll contact them," she said.

He nodded and then sat quietly, lost in deep thought. He mulled over and over what she had said. Her words of wisdom made sense and comforted him. He felt calm and composed.

"You've inherited your Granddad's mannerisms and his looks. You remind me so much of him and I'm confident you'll live up to his ideals. He always used to say, 'Remember three things and you can't go wrong: honesty, honor and courage, it doesn't matter who you're with or where you are in the world, it will always serve you well.' It seems to me that you are already applying those ideals from what you've told me so far."

"It's a tall order, but I'll try, Mata ji, I'll try."

There is, he supposed, no escaping the genes. That was why he was always looking out for other people and up for a good laugh.

"Bless you, dear, I know you will, now come, let's enjoy Ramu's cooking."

Jawali walked towards the kitchen and Naj began to lose himself in his thoughts. He was pleased that he had been able to share his concerns and worries. The weight had lifted off his shoulders as a result. She shuffled her way to the door and glanced back in his direction, but he was still sitting there motionless, lost. "Come on; hurry and get cleaned up," she called, with a nod towards the washroom.

Naj looked as though he wanted to stay a while longer, but suddenly he swung himself off the bed and rushed past her into the washroom.

"That's my boy," said Jawali.

Grandmother has amazing self-assurance and a lot of charm, he thought.

Jawali was a woman much involved in faith, with a deep interest in other people's welfare, especially those far less fortunate than herself, and there were many. She was always speaking on their behalf, always expressing sympathy. She often had little talks with God and had asked him to help protect the vulnerable, the weak, the destitute and, of course, the little orphans. God, of course, listened patiently and agreed to give it some thought. Jawali felt sure that things would change for the better in time. She told Naj that God was on the case.

A little talk with his Grandmother had been what Naj needed. It had been a perfect antidote for his low mood and, by God, it had worked instantly. He was a new man, a man with a smile on his face, and a spring in his step. He was rejuvenated, full of energy.

I'll go for a little run, Naj thought. *Yes; why not? I need to exercise my lungs.* Running was Naj's favorite way of keeping fit, a favorite pastime. And as a keen football player, running was something that had to be done regularly. He ran twice a week in the evening. In addition to his Tuesday evening training session with his team, he played regularly on Sunday. His body demanded a workout; he felt the need for the buzz that comes with it. Naj changed into his shorts and sweatshirt. It was a pleasant morning, he thought, as he limbered up on the patio. From the kitchen window, Jawali and Ramu watched him going through his gentle stretching exercises. She felt happy and proud. On seeing Naj doing his push-ups, Ramu began feeling his own biceps secretly. Naj was an athlete and had a body to match. Ramu felt envious of his physique. *I wish I had a body like that,* he thought. *Oh, Jesus look at his thighs, they are enormous, even bigger than the wrestler Mehsopuria Hukma Singh's, and his biceps are in better shape than those of Salman Khan.*

His muscles warmed up, Naj was ready for the run. He took a sip of water, rinsed his mouth, opened the gate and jogged out on the way to the military hospital, a tall, handsome young man with black sunglasses. His eyes scanned the unevenness of the earth beneath his feet. He jogged steadily, taking care not to injure himself in any way, avoiding potholes and debris on the ground as well as the oncoming traffic. The towering apartments to his left were home to many families and reminded him of the high rise flats in Stevenage back to the Bowes Lyons House Youth Project. Their dark, dingy concrete stairs rose to the seventh floor. They smelled of urine and were full of graffiti. Human beings were housed in their hundreds, like chickens in a battery farm. *Someday a brave and bold politician will come along and knock all these awful places down and replace them with decent housing to live in*, he thought.

Naj continued close to the kerb until he reached the hospital. *It must be about a mile and half from my gran's*, he thought. He stood looking across at the hospital building, breathing heavily. It was no different to any of the hospitals in England. Nurses and doctors were going about their business in their white uniforms. He spat to clear his throat, turned back and jogged past a roadside hut that was serving American-style hotdogs. The smell of the fried onions was tempting. He felt the urge to stop and indulge in a feast, fried onions covered with mustard. It had been a while since he'd eaten a hotdog, and it smelled so mouth-watering. He stopped, he looked, he licked his lips and realized he had no money on him, but promised to treat himself later that day. *Maybe I can send Ramu to come and buy one for me, he thought* as he jogged back home.

Later that afternoon, the fading sun of early evening cast changing patterns of light and shadow on the patio, chairs, table, plants and flower pots.

"Here; take this and go get me a hotdog." Naj thrust a one hundred rupee note towards Ramu as he sipped from a bottle of Diet Coke. The word "hotdog" reminded Ramu of a funny joke someone had told him recently, but before he could share it with Naj he began to laugh hysterically and fell over, smashing a large flower pot. When he realized what he'd done his laughter stopped abruptly. With a sinking feeling in the pit of his stomach he looked at his master and feared the worst. It would cost him half a month's wages to replace it and probably some harsh words to go with it. But rather than being angry and upset, Naj couldn't help but laugh at seeing Ramu on his backside amongst the flower beds. Ramu was surprised; he was now in no doubt that his new master was a man of extraordinary qualities.

CHAPTER FOUR

Naj had been in Cantonia for three days and had recuperated well. His stay in India was passing and he was getting impatient to explore the neighborhood and beyond. After breakfast he got dressed and headed out. He stood at the gate for a few moments, contemplating which direction to take. He looked left, then right and left again, as if he was about to cross a busy road. As the morning fog gradually disappeared and the sun began to shine, the temperature increased rapidly. Dressed in a t-shirt, blue jeans and sandals, he headed towards the main road. On the other side of the road, to the east, there was open ground about the size of three football pitches. It was fenced off in all four directions with two access points, one to the east and the other to the west. The ground, known as Dusshera Ground, had designated sections for different activities. There was a basketball area, a football pitch, and a play area for little children with slides, climbing frames and several swings. Here, boys of different ages played football, cricket, and basketball. Seasonally, gulli danda, kabadi and pithu pithu were enjoyed by many keen, ambitious participants. In addition, it also facilitated a number of different cultural, religious, political and sports events each year. These events were very popular and attracted large crowds. The locals, families, neighbors, adjoining villagers and soldiers all came in their thousands. Each year a Basant festival

(Guru Gobind Singh Ji's wedding anniversary and also a new season of spring) was held in the grounds. The locals donated funds towards the running costs as well as helping to run it. It gave a sense of belonging and pride to the area. The magic of the festival had to be seen to be believed. A colorful display of kites littered the sky and the young women swaying to the pulsating rhythm of gidda, displaying the vigor of the Land of the Five Rivers, were charming. Contemporary and traditional folk singers performed in the evening, taking centre-stage. The exuberant dance beats of the dhol electrified the atmosphere and brought the young bhangra-loving Panjabis to their feet, swaying their arms in the air, in ecstasy. The crowd stood and applauded the performers to acknowledge their well-rehearsed steps and talents.

Naj was staring at the ground when two boys of fourteen or fifteen walked past him, laughing, chattering, holding hands openly, like lovers do. A lorry driver sounded his horn and shouted "I love you darling," at them, and they laughed together at the same time. *Idiots,* he thought.

It was a splendid morning. Like a happy smile on a child's face, it touched the hearts of many. A car came to a stop nearby and two uniformed soldiers jumped out. One lit a cigarette, took a long draw and then puffed it out in rings as they turned towards the shops. Naj crossed the road and walked into the ground through the gate. As he stood there he remembered Ramu telling him about the wonderful spectacle of people gathered together, dressed in their best attire. It was always like a grand party. People from different castes, classes, religions and social groups all got together to participate and enjoy. There was always something happening at this ground; it was a real community hub for the locals. Naj walked around the ground and came across a boy about ten years of age, kicking a football by himself.

"Hey there, can anyone play?" said Naj, walking over to him.

The boy looked anxiously at Naj, but decided to kick the ball to him. Naj returned the favor and kicked it back.

"My name's Naj," he said, extending his hand as he got closer. The boy hesitated at first, and then took a small step forward and they shook hands.

"I'm Tinku, sir."

"Do you live around here, Tinku?"

"Over there, sir," said the boy, pointing towards a block of flats to the east. "How about you sir, where do you live? I mean I haven't seen you around here before."

"Oh, I'm just visiting, but my Grandmother lives over there." He pointed to Jawali's house.

"What number, sir?"

"Number 10."

"The little old lady who lives in that bungalow, is she your Grandmother?"

"Yes, that's her. Do you know her?"

"No. Yes, I mean, I don't know her by name, sir, but I know what she is like." Tinku had thought her a battle-axe since she caught him up her mango tree, trying to steal. He had been hungry and hadn't eaten since a day before. Realizing he might have said too much, he quickly put a hand over his mouth.

"What do you mean?" Naj looked at him and suddenly Tinku's eye twitched with fear. He quickly rolled the ball under his foot and leaned back as if to protect himself, and replied: "Oh nothing sir, she . . . she's just very old and fragile and . . . and I believe she lives alone with a servant," he answered slowly. "Sorry, I have to go, sir," said Tinku picking the ball up.

"Tinku, hold on a minute, please hold on. I didn't mean to alarm you in any way. I'm sorry, don't be scared; I'm new here and I like playing football. Is there anywhere I can have a kick-about with some local lads?"

"Oh, that's easy me and my friends play football here every day, usually after school. If you fancy a game with us, just turn up around four or four thirty, sir. But now I have to do something for my father." Tinku jogged towards the flats with the ball in his hands.

"OK, thanks. I'll see you later, Tinku."

With a football kick-about on his mind, Naj bought himself a pair of cheap football boots from a shop in the market place. He was excited about playing, and tried to picture himself living here for the rest of his life. *There are no pubs here,* he thought, *only liquor stores, and the beer tastes crap. No, it wouldn't be the same. I'd get bored with watching those awful Bollywood movies.*

The afternoon sun was going down quickly and his shadow shifted as he crossed the main road, and then vanished. He walked slowly at first and then broke into a steady run in order to warm up his leg muscles. He stopped dead on reaching a group of boys playing football. He heard their loud shouts and screams. The ground was dry, dusty and hard with potholes. He noticed a few boys playing without trainers or shoes.

"How can anyone play football on a ground like this with bare feet?" Naj murmured to himself. He looked for Tinku, but he was nowhere to be seen. He stood there observing, tackles were going in hard and there was a competitive edge to the game. He felt they were a little disorganized but appeared to be enjoying the game. *I could help them to organize a bit better and it may help them to improve their game,* he thought.

One of the boys caught his eye. Naj moved towards him with a smile.

"Are you looking for Tinku?" he asked.

"Yes, where is he?"

"He'll be along in a minute, he had to do something for his father."

"You want to play with us?"

"Yeah, that would be good."

"You played before?"

"Yes, a little."

"You are new here, aren't you, sir?"

"Yeah." The game stopped and all the boys came over and stood behind Bantoo.

"Tell us where you played before."

"England."

They laughed at him. "England, UK?"

"We never heard of an Indian footballer playing for England," a boy named Laloo said.

"No, I didn't play for England, I said I played *in* England. That's where I'm from. I'm not an Indian; I'm English and India is my ancestral home."

"What's 'ancestral home'?" asked a boy with a flat nose.

"So what position do you play?" another asked, looking at him.

"I play up front for my team, but I can play in any position."

The boys were impressed by his knowledge of the game and began to argue amongst themselves about whose side he should play for. Tinku arrived on the scene and the matter was resolved. Naj was put in the position of full-back on

Journey Home

Bantoo's team and Tinku agreed to play for the opposing side. The game started.

"Ramesh, over here," a skinny little kid screamed. He pumped the ball out to him in the centre of the field. Naj raced towards the ball and the skinny kid beat him to it. Naj put in a soft tackle but the boy whipped the ball past him. He then skipped around two more players, passed the goalkeeper and put the ball in the back of the net. He ran towards his team mates shouting: "They don't call me Ronaldo for nothing."

"Ronaldo, Ronaldo!" His team mates mobbed him. Within the next five minutes he had scored two more and at half-time the score was four nil. Gully and his team mates were distraught with the score.

"You told us you could play football," said Bantoo. "The boys want you off the team; you're not much good are you?"

"I can play football no problem, but you're all so tiny I'm scared I might end up hurting one of you with my tackles."

"You are a liar; we've seen you play and you can't even stop Motoo and he's rubbish."

"OK, OK, just give me five minutes more and I'll prove it to you all," he said.

They agreed to keep him on their side after a brief conference amongst themselves. Naj knew that this was his only chance to impress them and make amends for his poor play. The game restarted and the skinny kid, now full of confidence, went to go past Naj with an easy shrug of the shoulders. Naj put in a hard challenge, took the ball from him and pumped it out to the winger Raju who played it back to Naj in one two fashion. He cut inside taking the full-back with him. He twisted and then flicked the ball over the goalkeeper into the empty net, as cool as you like. He was mobbed by his team mates. Within the next ten minutes he scored another three goals with ease, levelling the score to four all. Everyone was mesmerized by his skills and trickery. Naj had acquired instant hero status amongst his new friends. Now the score was level he felt it was time for him to leave: "I'm sorry guys, I've got to go."

"Show us that trick you did before you go, sir," Motoo said.

"Which one?"

"That one where you flicked the ball over your head from behind."

"Tomorrow, I promise."

"Can we call for you tomorrow, sir?"

"Don't worry, I'll be here on time," said Naj reassuringly.

Word got around very quickly amongst the serious footballers and a few older boys from the neighborhood came to watch him play at the following session. They were also impressed by his knowledge, skills, and trickery with the ball. They told him about a competition between the Khalsa College and the Military Unit. He was asked to play for them and he agreed. He knew he was short on fitness and began to train hard for the game. His training program consisted of jogging for two miles early in the morning, followed by half-hour exercises, a mid-day session practicing with the ball for an hour and then playing with his team in the evening. He only had four days to get ready and prove his worth to the team; with that in mind he trained every minute he could spare.

Harjit Singh, the college team's captain, came to see Naj at his home and told him that he would be wearing the number 9 shirt and would play in the centre forward position. Naj was very pleased. Harjit also emphasized the importance of the competition to him and said he must play for the team and not only for himself. They talked about tactics and how the match might be played.

"I promise to give one hundred percent for the team, and if I fail to perform by half-time, take me off," Naj said, adding, "Mind you, if we get on top I'll want to play the full ninety minutes." Naj was not fully fit but that wasn't going to stop him from giving his best for the Khalsa. After all, they were taking a chance on him as well as letting him wear the famous number 9 shirt.

The match between the Military Unit and Khalsa College received a lot of publicity and hundreds turned up for the match. Khalsa College wore a traditional all-saffron strip. They had brought two coach-loads of supporters with them. When the teams took the field those fans began to chant, "Khalsa, Khalsa, Khalsa . . . a . . . chakday . . ." Seated in the front row, Jawali also joined in the sing song, "Chakday, chakday, chakday Khalsa . . ."

Harjit got all his players into a circle and they all linked arms with each other, and then said a little prayer.

"The cup belongs to us, it's got Khalsa written all over it. You hear me, dostoe?" said Harjit.

"Yeah," they replied.

"I didn't hear you," said he raising his voice.

"The cup belongs to Khalsa," they shouted at top of their lungs, their supporters joining in.

"Let's show them what we're made of. Give it all you've got, so come on, let's do it."

The referee summoned the captains to the centre circle and tossed a coin that decided who would start the game. They shook hands and Khalsa kicked at the referee's whistle. Ranjit passed the ball to Dev and darted upfield. Dev slipped it to Taroo who was waiting at the right wing. Taroo hesitated and failed to collect the ball, and the military's centre-forward charged at him, mowing him down. Taroo screamed as he rolled around on the ground in pain. The referee blew his whistle as he came running waving his hand.

"Off, off, off," the crowd roared. "Send him off ref, send him off!"

The Khalsa players surrounded the referee. Naj rushed over to see if he could help. Their trainer came on to the field and attended to Taroo's injury. He was helped off the field to recover and came back on after a treatment. In the meantime, the offender was punished with a warning and a yellow card. Khalsa players took some time to settle down after the incident, but soon began to pass the ball around with confidence. The ball was now in the opposing side of the field with Ashok slipping it sideways to Naj, who tricked past his marker with a quick shuffle and beat the second defender as he put the ball back into the net. The goalie had no chance and didn't see it until it was too late. The Khalsa players and their supporters were elated. Jawali couldn't help but wave her arms about in the excitement, while the little boy and his friends jumped up down as they chanted "Naj, Naj, Naj!" Naj jumped for joy and ran back to the centre-circle with his arms held up in triumph. Scoring a goal boosted Naj's confidence. The game continued and both sides battled for the ball. Fouls were committed regularly and players disciplined. The referee let the game flow until Shah, a military player, put in a double-footed tackle and sent Naj flying, with only fifty seconds remaining on the clock before half-time. His boot had caught Naj on the ankle and he screamed in pain. The referee instantly showed Shah a red card and he was off.

Journey Home

Naj's ankle was already beginning to swell and he limped off the field with help from the trainer. Naj was angry with the referee for not sending Shah off for a similar tackle on him some five minutes earlier. There was no hope of Naj playing in the second half and he sat frustrated, holding an ice pack to his ankle.

The score at half-time remained the same, one nil to Khalsa. With the advantage of one extra player on their side, the Khalsa supporters were confident in winning the cup. The teams returned for the second half. Sodhi replaced Naj and the coach changed the system from 4-4-2 to 4-5-1, surprising everyone. Both sides began with enthusiasm, determined to score first. Khalsa were keen to increase their lead and the Military Unit aimed for an equalizer. Both sides fought like lions. The Military Unit had to work extra hard but they never gave up trying to level the score. The clock ticked away and the score stayed the same. Both sets of players were tiring because of the harsh conditions on the pitch and the extremely high temperature. It wasn't long before fatigue set in and a number of players began dropping on the ground like flies, with cramps. There were casualties all over the pitch and the neutrals were calling for the game to be stopped. With just two minutes to go to full-time the game almost came to a standstill. Military Unit kept trying to level the score and Khalsa College were desperately hanging on to their precious one nil lead. The last few minutes became like hours for the players, someone threw a smoke bomb on the field and players ran for cover. The referee blew his final whistle and the game came to an end. Khalsa were jubilant, thanks to their hero Naj and the first half goal scored by him, and Military Unit's players and supporters distraught. The Panjab police was quick on the scene wielding their long sticks at the demonstrators and soon had the situation under control.

The next day, a crowd of local well wishers, including his junior team mates, arrived early at Jawali's gate. "Naj, Naj, Naj . . . hero, hero!" they chanted continuously. Ramu was ordered to calm them down, but no, they insisted their hero show his face. The Tribune, a local newspaper, ran his story and everyone connected with football was talking about him. Two men from the Panjab Football Federation Board turned up unannounced at Jawali's house, with a view to him playing for them. They were disappointed when they learned that he was a British passport holder and had no desire to play for them even if he had been eligible to do so.

CHAPTER FIVE

"Take Ramu with you. He knows the area as well as anyone. In fact, he knows it inside out, as he's lived here all of his life," Naj's Grandmother said.

"It's OK; I'll find my way around, and if I'm not back in a couple of hours don't forget to send out a search party for me," said Naj, smiling.

"Be careful now, and mind the traffic when you're crossing the road."

"Don't worry, Grandmother. I will stick to the green cross code."

"What code?"

"Oh nothing, I was just joking." Naj took out his cell phone and began checking for messages, then stared as Ramu set a cup of coffee in front of him.

"What did you say, beta? I didn't hear you properly," she said slowly scratching her forehead.

"It was nothing Grandma, nothing at all." He lifted the cup, put it to his lips and took a sip as he thought about what to wear. Then he rose, leaving the empty cup on the table, and went to his bedroom to change into a fresh set of clothes. "I should be back by lunch-time, Ramu. Tell Grandmother not to worry."

He stood at the roadside with his sunglasses on, his eyes wandering over the grounds across the road, looking for his young football team players. There were none. It was a pleasant sunny morning with a light breeze. It hadn't rained for a while and the surface of the road was dry and dusty. The heavy traffic rushing by made the dust rise up to his face. A deadly mixture of dust and fumes made him feel slightly stuffy and he needs to clear his nostrils. He took a handkerchief from his pocket and blew his nose into it violently.

Naj had been at the road for less than a minute when a rickshaw man pulled up in front of him and said, "Can I take you anywhere, sir?" He'd never been on a rickshaw in his life before. *Why not?* He thought.

"How much do you charge?" he asked the man.

"Where do you wish to go, sir?"

"Nowhere in particular," replied Naj.

The man looked at him in amazement and smiled. "Why do you rich people like making a mockery of us poor?"

Naj was distressed by the poor man's comment. "What do you mean? How am I making a mockery of you? Explain yourself!" Naj demanded.

The man looked questioningly at his designer jeans and t-shirt. "You say you're not sure where you wish to go, but you prefer to waste my time and make fun of me all the same."

"No, no, no, I'm not making fun of you. You got me all wrong," he pleaded. "I'm just not sure where I should be going." The man gave him a hard glare, spat on the ground and pushed off.

Naj shouted at him to stop: "Take me with you!"

The man pulled up some yards ahead and looked back at him, confused. Naj mounted the vehicle taking his seat.

"Let me ask you again sir, where do you wish to go? No, I'll rephrase the question. Where do you want me to take you, sir?"

"Take me . . . Just take me around the area. I just want to see what there is to see."

A strange customer, he thought. Normally his customers knew where they wished to go, but this man wasn't sure about where he wanted to go. He found him odd and thought he might be high on drugs.

"I take it you have the means to pay for your ride?"

"Of course I have," Naj assured him.

"Please don't take it the wrong way, sir. You see, some people get to their destination and then refuse to pay, that's all I'm saying, sir. I have been robbed of my services many times in the past and I have to be sure that my customer has the means on them."

"Don't worry about the fare, just tell me how much you'll charge me for a two hour hire."

"Two hours, how about two hundred rupees, sir; that's a good price on a hot day like this."

Naj quickly converted a hundred rupees into English money in his head. It came to two pounds and fifty pence. *That's not bad for a two hour ride,* he thought.

"OK, agreed. You'll get your two hundred rupees once two hours are up." He checked his watch for time. "It's just gone ten past eleven on my watch and at ten past one you'll get your money. Now let's go."

This man must be an NRI [non-resident of India] *or just stupid to pay me two hundred rupees for two hours' work without haggling. I usually only make that much on a good day*, the rickshaw man thought.

Naj felt like a lord of the manor seated behind the poor skinny rickshaw man. The driver pushed down on the pedals with all his might and moved forward slowly, avoiding the potholes and the oncoming traffic.

"Tell me," Naj said, resting his hand on the man's shoulder. "How much do these things cost to buy? This thing would look cool in my backyard. I can imagine me and my mate Tom riding back and forth to the pub." *Yeah, it'll save me lot of legwork,* Naj thought. *I'll get Tom to ride it and I'll sit on the back seat like this.*

"These things cost a lot of money, sir, a lot of money. I bought this five years ago and I'm still paying for it. To be honest, if I had the money I'd buy myself a car, sir. With a taxi, one can earn ten times as much as with this blood-thirsty push-pedal" said the man, raising his voice against the roar of traffic.

It was so nice to be out in the sunshine in the fresh air as Naj sat high above the ground looking about, observing freely without a care in the world and with plenty of time on his hands.

"Do you mind if I ask you another question?" said Naj, leaning forward and raising his voice.

"No, go ahead, ask what you like, it's your time, sir."

A heavy goods vehicle sounded its horn, and overtook them by forcing them off the tarmac.

"Go fuck yourself !" the man shouted at the lorry driver and showed him his middle finger.

"Do you enjoy your job as a rickshaw man?" Naj was trying to understand the lives of people like him, people he didn't know much about. What made them take up rickshaw service?

"Why do you ask, sir?" he replied, looking anxiously at the oncoming traffic.

"I'm just curious, that's all.

Journey Home

The man looked back over his shoulder, making a face: "You're kidding me. Happiness is only for people with money; it's not for the likes of me. We poor people have no time for happiness, we're always chasing our tails, always looking for the next rupee in order to feed our families." A lone cloud crossed the sun, casting a shadow over Cantonia. "Since you ask, sir, let me tell you about living in poverty. I have a three-year-old baby and she is lying sick in bed this very minute and I have no money to pay for the medicine she needs and you're asking me if I'm happy being a rickshaw man. People in my situation don't have a life, our lives are often worse than that of a working donkey. At least they get time off for rest. My life is twenty-four-seven and I'm on the lookout for the next customer even when I'm totally exhausted. I can't afford to say no, because I need the money. If I don't work, I'm doomed to starve, starve my family to death as well. What's the life of one rickshaw man? What does it matter? How does it matter? Why does it matter? There are thousands of us providing cheap, useful transportation for thousands, millions across India. Often I don't even go home and just take a nap on the back seat."

They came to a stop. He pulled up by the roadside and wiped the sweat off his face and neck and coughed, spitting inhaled muck and dust from the back of his throat. Naj was moved, profoundly moved. Before he had the chance to compose himself, the man questioned him: "How old do you think I am, sir?" he said, turning his face towards Naj.

"Oh God, I don't know. I'm not very good at that kind of thing," said Naj.

"Go on, have a guess, sir."

"Alright, I'll try, but promise you won't accuse me of making a mockery of your situation."

"No, I won't, sir, I promise."

Naj scanned the hard lines across the man's forehead and around his eyes. His head was covered in dust, he had blackened teeth and his moustache and sideburns were mostly white.

"I would guess you're about forty-five or maybe nearer fifty."

The man found this amusing and fell over laughing. "Fifty!" he laughed hysterically.

"What's so funny?"

"Funny, it's the best joke I've heard in years, sir," he said laughing. "Fifty? For your information, sir, even my Dad isn't fifty yet. Mind you, he'll be fifty in December, thank God, which reminds me I have to save up for a bottle of good rum. He likes a drop of rum now and then, it helps him with his rheumatoid problems. He is one of the luckiest ones in my family to be alive at his age. Normally they die much, much earlier. My uncles, all three of them, they died in succession, one after another. Uncle Mota, the elder of the three, died at the age of forty-two and the other two followed him a year later, within two weeks of each other. You see, sir, it's our lifestyle. We can't afford to eat healthily on our tiny income, then it's this damn machine. Although it provides us with the opportunity to earn a little bit of money, pushing the pedals up and down on the dirt roads, carrying heavy passengers day and night is a real killer."

Naj straightened up. *How strange,* he thought. *How odd this meeting, this getting together with a total stranger under the shadow of the lone cloud connecting us. What could be the purpose? What powers could be behind this? First I met Sonia, a total stranger and now, another stranger, the rickshaw man. Odd, very odd.* Indeed, it was as if some mystical powers had planned his journey home.

"You see, sir," the man said. "We have to survive somehow and this is the only way. I'll take whatever comes my way to earn a few rupees legally. I'll take the customer wherever they wish to go as long as they pay me fairly. Me, I was born into poverty. I'm poor, degradingly poor. Like I said before, there's no way out for me. I can't read or write, I don't have skills that can pay me better wages. That's it, this is all I know, so I'm stuck with it. Sometimes I think that God must have a grudge against the poor. And for the poor that means a never-ending circle of struggle and pain until the last breath. Some well-off people will tell you that the poor are poor because they are put on this earth for a purpose. They are here to endure suffering for others. Personally, I think that's rubbish. There are those who argue that knowledge comes through suffering, and that might be true, but my family, including myself, have had more than our share already and I can't see an end to this misery." He pushed hard on the pedal and sounded his horn to overtake a bullock cart. Bitterly, he continued: "I pity the rich. In my view they are worthless. I pity and despise them because they are too greedy and they don't like sharing with the likes of me. They'd rather waste it than give it to people like myself. It is a sad thing and they are sad people. I'm a religious man and I don't mean harm to anyone. If I was honest, I would say I feel sorry for them deep down." There was a dignity about this man. He was poor and struggled to survive, proud and respectable, which Naj admired. Embarrassing him was the last thing he wished to do.

The sun continued to climb and the temperature soared. Within minutes it became extremely hot. It was hot enough to melt the skin off one's bones. The man was soon drenched in his own sweat. The dust blew constantly into his nostrils and he struggled to breathe. He coughed hard like a person suffering with bronchitis, but kept on going, kept pushing, stuck to his duties unselfishly.

"Why don't we rest for a while under a shade or something?" said Naj.

"I'll stop if you want me to as long as you pay me for my time," he said abruptly, and stared back at him. "I need to carry on working, earn rupees, to buy food, clothes, medicine for my family. I can't afford to stop. You see, our lives are like a dry river bed, waiting, looking for that next drop of rain. Rain provides life, money provides life. As I said before, sir, my little girl is very, very sick and I don't have the means to pay for medicine. You get my point, sir?"

"Tell you what I'll do, how about I treat you to an ice cold drink?"

They stopped at a store by the cinema. For now the driver could rest. He relaxed, took a piece of cloth out of his pocket and wiped his face with it, then carefully dusted the rickshaw seats. They sat down under a pipal tree, flicked open the cans and took a long drink. There were a dozen or so other people there, sitting, standing, laughing and talking; "Chakdey, chakdey," a tune by Digital Delay, was playing in the background.

"This is the only luxury I look forward to on a hot day, sipping on an ice cold drink under the shade of a tree. It has to be a kind of magic, thank you, sir, thank you so much. I didn't mean to be disrespectful in any way, nor was I trying to put you down," said the man.

Naj could see that he meant every word. "It's OK, no harm done. Forget about it. You have taught me a great deal in a short time."

"Sir, you know what, you're the kindest man I have met in a long time. I have met many who took pleasure in abusing me because of my situation, but you, sir, are a rare breed if I may say so."

"Thank you, thank you for the kind words yourself," replied Naj as he sat back into his seat. They were ten minutes into their journey when they came to a steep hill and the man almost came to a stop. He climbed down from his seat and began pushing the rickshaw on foot. Naj felt so sorry for him that he too jumped down and started to help him push.

"Sir, please get back on the seat, I'll be all right, it's this hill," said the man. Naj felt very guilty and sorry for the man. He himself was now covered in dust and sweat also poured off his body. He looked at the man and felt disgusted with himself. He was witnessing the other side of life, the human suffering caused by poverty. His perception of a decent, good life had completely changed.

The trip over, Naj gave the man ten pounds of English money for his troubles and wished him farewell with a hug, turned and made his way back on foot, distraught and angry, thinking about the man's situation and his suffering. This was a real experience in a real situation. Not made up, not invented or set up like a film set. It was real, something more that touched him deep inside, that moved him. It was odd, but genuine.

The next day began on a positive note. The sun came up early, the birds were singing outside in the garden. Naj spoke to Lucy on the phone. She told him she missed him and he told her how much he loved her. He scanned the local English newspaper, took a shower and enjoyed his breakfast on the patio. He decided to go for a walk, told his Grandmother he'd be back in a little while and suggested she enjoy the morning sun. She sat on the patio minding her own business, a formidable old lady. Ramu had picked a handful of fresh flowers from the garden and quickly put them in a vase and presented it to her.

"Take them inside and put them on the dining table, they'll brighten the room no end," she said.

Everything was fine until Naj went for that walk. Afterwards, he came home, had a shower and changed his clothes and sat there looking glum. He didn't eat much. He flicked the pages of a magazine or two, then wandered off to the shops with no interest in buying anything, although the shopkeepers did their best to entice him with all sorts of discounts. He returned, still preoccupied with his earlier experience and thoughts. The afternoon was no better. He grew more and more gloomy, not about the rickshaw man; about everything. That evening he went to bed early with thoughts of his rickshaw trip fresh on his mind which, coupled with the heat, made it impossible for him to sleep properly, even with the ceiling fan spinning above him. Tossing and turning, with dogs barking and howling in the distance and mosquitoes droning over his netted bed, he made a promise to himself that he would never ride on a rickshaw again unless it was operated by an engine. A wave of pity and compassion for the rickshaw people surged in him. He wished there was something he could do for them and their situation, but the task was too great for one man; the thought mocked him. Suddenly he felt a wave of anger rising at the system and the politicians alike for not doing enough to alleviate poverty.

The following morning Naj was up early, the man's stories still singing in his ears. He didn't feel the need for breakfast. He needed to think, he needed to talk to someone who understood humanity, someone with wisdom, someone with a listening ear, to share, to understand. Where could he go? Who could he talk to? Grandmother wasn't feeling herself and Ramu, no, he had his own problems with poverty. Maybe Mrs. Datta? No, she wouldn't be interested unless she was going to get something out of it. Who else, who else indeed? Naj felt restless and in pain. He moved round and round in a circle, like a dog chasing its tail, frustrated. It was still early in the morning and the sound of prayers filtered into his bedroom through the window. An answer to his question was there and then it came to him. *I know*, he thought. He took a shower and headed to the temple. Men, women, children, everyone was going about their business. There was the noise of the traffic and humming birds moving among branches. A pack of stray dogs followed a bitch on heat. The temple was a short distance from the bungalow. Naj walked quietly and arrived within a matter of minutes. He knew what he had to do. He was on a mission. He removed his shoes, washed his hands, rang the bell and slowly walked into the main hall. There he asked the lord to pay special attention to the plight of the poor and to end all disparities between the rich and the poor, not just in India but across the globe. In the past, Naj might have not been a believer, but he had been taken by surprise by moments of extraordinary exaltation since arriving in his ancestral home. He began to realize that everything had a purpose and what happens, happens for a reason. It was conceivable that there were greater powers out there determining our journey on this planet, from the beginning to the end.

CHAPTER SIX

"I must show you those photographs of your Mum and Dad's wedding that I promised you," said Jawali with her most motherly smile. "There are only four remaining now, I don't know what happened to the other two." She went to her room and came out clutching a small paper box in her hand, all wrapped up neatly in a red cloth. "Here they are," she said, taking her seat. Naj came and sat down beside her. She put the box in front of her and sat looking at it for a moment. "This box hasn't seen the light of the day for at least fifteen years," she said.

A smile flashed across his face. "Fifteen years?" He looked at the box closely and said, "That explains it, that's why it's all covered in dust."

"Covered in dust, where?" She rubbed it with her fingers and then held the hand close to her face. "I can't see any dust," she protested. Her eyesight was beginning to fail, even with the aid of her spectacles, but she wouldn't have any of it. "Where's the dust? Show me; I've had this box all locked up in a trunk under the bed and there's no way any dust could've got in there," she said. He said nothing, as he didn't wish to hurt her feelings. She began to untie the knot. Her fingers hadn't the strength, but she kept trying.

"Here, let me do it, Grandma."

"These damn hands are getting more useless by the day," she conceded, holding them in front of her. He removed the cloth and put it to one side.

"Give it to me, beta." She lifted the lid. She was so focused on the box and its contents that she hadn't noticed her white cashmere shawl slipping off her shoulders onto her lap.

Naj leaned over, his eyes fixed on a photograph that she was holding.

"That is your Dada ji," she said, taking a deep breath. They studied the photograph, and the room fell silent. Suddenly, a lone tear ran down her cheek. He did not notice, he was so consumed by the black and white image in front of him. He was fascinated by it; he just sat there looking at it.

"He looks so grand and brave. You have to tell me everything about him," he insisted.

She swallowed hard and then wiped the tear off her face. "I will beta, I promise," she said sadly.

"Who's this standing next to Granddad? No, don't tell me, let me guess," he laughed. "Oh my God, it can't be?" They looked at each other.

"You've guessed right, that's your father," she said.

Naj's eyes glowed. "Oh man, he looks so cool with his little turban." Naj was amused but proud. She looked at his smiling face and felt happy. "Can I borrow this photograph, Grandma?" he asked cheerfully. "I'll get a copy made and take it back to England." *I'll show it to Tom and Lucy,* he thought. *My old man in a turban, wicked!*

"Of course, beta, but don't lose it. I have already lost two, and they are priceless to me." She said.

"I'll look after it with my life, I promise it won't leave my sight, not even for a minute."

Outside, the sun was climbing and it was getting hot. Life has a way of surprising everyone from time to time. Today an old photo of his father had surprised Naj. In a million years, he could not have imagined seeing his Dad wearing a turban. He couldn't get over it, his old man, whom he had only seen in a bobble hat in winter, wearing a turban!

"Can we talk about Granddad now, what was he like?" he said leaning forward in his chair.

She glanced up. "Your Grandfather," she said, "was one of the kindest and handsomest men one could meet in a lifetime. Everyone admired him for his thoughtfulness and honesty. There were a few who envied him, I have to say." Her mind wandered for a moment and she asked: "Where was I?"

"You were telling me about Granddad," said Naj, reaching across the seat and patting her hand.

"Silly me, I don't know what's happening to me lately, I lose track of things halfway. Now, your Grandfather, he had everything, the looks, the height, the smile. He knew the meaning of the world." She seemed remarkably proud.

A motor horn sounded out in the street. The birds chattered in a queer harmony out by the window. Naj inspected the photo and a smile came to his face: "He was tall, wasn't he, Grandmother?"

"Yes, he was tall," answered Jawali, with a sudden brightening of her face, like a moon emerging from behind a dark cloud.

"And here is your mother Jeeti; doesn't she look like a princess in that red sari? I had to go to Ludhiana for that. Your Great Massi Dhano and I caught an early morning bus from Rama Mandi and didn't get back until six in the evening. We went from shop to shop in the Bheerha bazaar.

Journey Home

We almost gave up until we saw this little shop tucked away in a corner. It was the first sari the shopkeeper showed us and we looked at each other and knew instantly that this was the one for your mother. Mind you, we had to haggle over the price with him and that took some negotiation, but that's nothing new in India. After half an hour we came out, feeling pleased with ourselves. We had got what we came for and at a reasonable cost. One thing my mother taught me was that you never pay the asking price, never; you keep haggling until you get it down to what you want to pay. The shopkeepers are so cunning they will always start at two or three times its real value. It all depends on who they're dealing with. They have one price for the locals and a much higher rate for the NRI. The outsiders always get ripped off, every time.

"What's 'NRI' Grandmother? I'm not familiar with this word?"

"NRI, those who live outside India, abroad."

"You mean people like me?"

"Yes, beta."

"I'm not an NRI, I'm English and very proud of it. I don't like this term and don't want people to call me 'NRI'. I find it very offensive and degrading. Whoever came up with this term should have his head tested. Indians who chose to live abroad make a massive contribution to the Indian economy. For instance, my Mum and Dad were born here and, as far as I'm concerned, they are Indian through and through, not 'NRI'. Yes, they are living in England, but what difference does that make? They have Indian passports and a home here. On top of all that, they have been sending money over for the last twenty years. So when they come home people refer to them as outsiders? That's totally unjust. How do you feel about this term 'NRI', Grandmother?"

"I don't know, beta, it's what everybody else is saying. I've heard it on the radio and on television many times and no one said they disapproved or questioned it like you. I think you are over-sensitive and over-critical about the whole thing. It's only a term, a name dear."

"Grandma, it's not just a name, it's much more than that, you wouldn't understand, it's offensive."

"Ramu, come here, beta," Jawali called out.

"Yes, Mata ji."

"Go and make tea for us."

"Yes, Mata ji."

He is too intellectual, too sensitive, he has adopted his Grandfather's attitude, she thought. *A cup of nice tea always did the trick, helped calm him down. Maybe it'll work some magic on Naj.* But Naj maintained his view about the issue of the 'NRI'.

Ramu was quick with the tea and set the cups down: "Is there anything else you require from me before I go back to my digging, Mata ji?"

"No."

Ramu left the room. She seized the moment and thought it was time to put her theory about the tea to the test.

"Beta, drink your tea before it goes cold." She hoped that he would drop the subject. It was a quarter past three. Naj looked at his watch, football practice on his mind. He lifted the cup and took a sip. A rhythmic, brass sound drifted from a nearby street.

"What's that sound, Grandmother?" he asked.

"Oh that, it's nothing."

Naj put the cup down and stood up. "It sounds like a live jazz practice of some sort." The sound was coming closer and closer by the second.

"Sit down, beta, it's nothing."

Now the sound was coming from the direction of the Dusshera ground. His curiosity made him go to see it for himself. He slipped on his trainers and rushed outside. He stood at the road and could see them coming towards him. There were others waiting, looking as they passed by. He saw a funeral procession led by a uniformed brass band. The tune they played was not familiar, but it was played in synchronization and in the spirit of the occasion. It seemed strange and unfamiliar. He had never seen anything like it in real life. The whole scene reminded him of a film he'd once seen about South American people.

Back inside, Jawali was looking at photographs still. "Here, beta, look; that's Dhano, my younger sister." He glanced over her shoulder. "She was so tall and beautiful. Sadly she died giving birth to her first child, a year after she was married. She was only sixteen at the time. She was a lovely sister. We were very close and she always looked to me for advice." She held the photo in both hands and put it against her chest. He quickly put his arm around her and sat holding her. She wiped a tear with one end of her duputta.

"Silly old me," she said. "I'm shedding tears like a child in front of my own grandson, that's not right." Suddenly, her black and white cat strolled in without a sound and rubbed against her leg. She wasn't alarmed. The cat had gone through this ritual many times. She knew it was her. She was familiar with her scent. The cat slowly moved over to inspect Naj. It lowered its head and sniffed him quickly, making him jump up in panic. He looked down on the floor and there she was looking straight at him with her big blue eyes, her tail in the air.

"Damn cat, go away!" Naj cried. He had never liked cats. They gave him the frights. He associated them with black magic and evil. For an odd moment his mind took him back to his East End bedsit. Whenever he looked out his window he saw a black cat looking back at him from the graveyard. He ended up living in semidarkness with the curtains drawn. The cat jumped onto the sofa and curled up next to his Grandmother.

"You know I don't like cats, Mata ji, make her go away" he protested.

"She's harmless, I don't know why you don't make friends with her. Besides, she is one of the family. I've had her since she was only a week old. You know, she understands everything," she continued. "She knows we are talking about her." The cat opened her eyes and looked at her. "You are a smart cat, aren't you, my little baby?" she said, stroking her gently.

"Please, tell her to go away," said Naj.

Jawali's eyebrows rose in dismay. The cat jumped down from the sofa, raised her tail and walked out of the room. Relief rushed through Naj.

"See what you've done, you've made her cross now!" Jawali cried.

"She's all right, Grandmother, she'll survive."

She didn't want to antagonize him by going on about her cat, but wished he treated Shaanti with a little kindness.

"Who is this, Mata ji?" Naj said looking at the last photograph.

"Oh that's your Mama ji, Sukhwinder."

"Ah . . . so that's Mama ji Sukhwinder. I've heard so much about him from Mum and Dad. They told me he was a brilliant footballer and a pilot in the army." An image formed in his mind, of Sukhwinder scoring the winning goal against China for India in the final of the Asian Games.

As a close relative and a keen football player himself, this gave Naj a sense of pride.

"Yes, he was good at most things, my little boy."

"Is it true, Mata ji, he was killed in the war with China?"

"That's true, mere putter." She leaned against her armrest, slightly emotional. There was sadness in her voice. "He was coming up to his twenty-fifth birthday when he was shot down over Amritsar, and what made it worse was that his body was never recovered. Damn wars, I have never understood the reason for them. Why can't people sit around the table and sort out their differences, instead of killing one another?"

He realized she still carried the pain of Sukhwinder's death, and his hand gently stroked her wrist. Naj's other hand crept up her cheek and brushed a tear away.

"I can see you are still hurting, Grandma," he whispered. It saddened him to see her like that. In order to snap her out of it he held the last photo to her face and said, "Who is that standing next to Mama ji?"

"That's me, silly."

"You look so young there," he said, grinning.

"I wasn't always this age. I was young once, I'll have you know."

"Look at those big eyes; they glitter like diamonds."

"Basharam,[shameless]" she said beaming Naj a smile. "Thank you, beta, thank you for the kind words. I didn't expect anything less from my own grandson," she said, glancing at him. There was a pause. Naj gripped her hand and gave her a warm smile, making the bond between them even stronger. He stood up and slid his hands into his pockets.

"Oh, Naj beta, before you go. We have some important guests arriving tomorrow and I want you looking your best for them."

"Don't worry, Grandmother. I won't let you down."

Naj was very tired and went to bed early. He slept. He dreamed almost at once. He was in his East End bedsit making love to Lucy. It was a short dream of extraordinary vividness and most enjoyable. He woke to find his Grandmother's cat nibbling at his face. He was so disappointed and upset that it had been a dream because the experience had been so real for him. The cat shrieked and shot out of the room when Naj threw the clock at it. He got out of bed, went to the washroom and cleaned up, then went into the kitchen and poured himself a glass of water. He stood in front of the window drinking. The sky was glittering with thousands of stars and in that brightness he could smell the scented air from the garden. He smiled as he thought about his friends in England. *If they could see me now. This is what I call paradise. Poor bastards are probably feeling the chill even with the central heating on full blast. Here I am down to my underwear trying to keep cool and the likes of Tom back home will be curling up under several layers of covers trying to keep warm.*

Naj noticed Ramu strolling around in the garden with a cigarette in his right hand, putting it to his mouth for a long draw. *Maybe he too had a dream like mine and couldn't sleep, the poor bastard*, he thought. Ramu was a tireless worker and carried out his duties with total commitment and passion. He never needed telling. He was one of those fellows who knew everything. He also knew his place with Mata ji and was proud to be employed by her. She had taken him on when he was only thirteen years. She had always treated him fairly. He had his own quarters in the grounds

Journey Home

next to the house and was a live-in worker. He ate, slept and worked at the Dulaks' house twenty-four-seven and had a day off per calendar month to spend with his family. His food and clothing were all paid for and he received a payment of 10,000 rupees annually into his parents' bank account. Once, she had loaned him 30,000 rupees when his family needed the money for his sister's wedding. He owed so much to her and would do anything for her without hesitation.

Naj had been restless for some reason. He couldn't put his finger on it. He was trying to work it out in his head. The more he investigated, the more he was unsure. It was a stuffy night even with the fan spinning above his bed. He was sweating, outside it was peaceful. There was the occasional sound of a dog howling in the distance, but other than that nothing but the sound of crickets drumming in his ear. He thought about taking a shower or having a cool bottle of beer. Scratching his head, Naj wandered around his room. Ramu was out of sight. *Maybe he's gone back to bed,* he thought. It was almost midnight on his watch. He was wide awake with nothing to do. His mind wandering from topic to topic, he went back to bed. Suddenly, Naj flashed back to the awful coach crash when he'd nearly lost his life. The scars were still sore and painful and the trauma recurred now and then when he was alone.

Two hours had passed when he glanced at his watch again. Frustrated, he went to the kitchen and came back with a can of cold beer. He sat on the edge of his bed and slowly drank and then returned to bed, hoping to get some sleep. He lay there wide awake, his mind wandering back to a different topic this time, to his teenage years. He must have been twelve or thirteen at the time, when suddenly it started to happen. It took him by surprise at first. He found it enjoyable and satisfying each time it happened. He would go to bed and then in his sleep "it" would come, come often, three or four times a week, without warning, while he dreamed. He didn't know what it was called, but it was a wonderful feeling until he felt the wetness in his underwear. He hated getting up to clean himself. He couldn't talk to his Mum, he couldn't talk to his Dad. It's not the sort of thing you talk to your parents about. It's embarrassing. His friends didn't talk about it. Yes, they talked about kissing, cuddling, hugging, breasts, masturbating and shagging, but never about wet dreams. This went on until his mother found out by chance when he kept asking for clean sheets night after night. She told Darsh about finding stains on the sheets and suggested he speak to the boy. Darsh had no idea how to approach the matter, as it was embarrassing for him. After many days he eventually plucked up enough courage and spoke to Naj in a roundabout way that was both funny and embarrassing. Naj told Tom who was going through the same experience, but whose mother had explained it in much simpler terms. She said it was normal for boys of his age and he'd nothing to worry about. They both had a good laugh talking about it afterward. The cockerel had begun to crow before Naj finally dropped off to sleep.

Next morning the clouds rolled all the way to Chandigharh. Before the sun broke though, Naj opened his eyes, bursting for a pee. He rushed to the bathroom and relieved himself. Ramu's delicious cooking smells filled the air. He could detect spicy aloo, and gobee-stuffed parathas. He was so hungry that he ate before taking a shower. At noon, Naj popped next door to Mrs. Datta's house for a chat.

"Come and sit down, Naj putter," she said, amiably. He perched rather than sat, making her think of an eagle ready

Journey Home

to take off at any time. She also seated herself uneasily on the edge of the chair.

"Make yourself comfortable, beta. What would you like to drink? Something hot or something cold?"

"I'm fine, thank you," he replied, leaning back into his seat.

"Have something, it's no trouble, really."

"OK, if you insist, something cold please."

"Let's see what we've got in the fridge," she said, getting to her feet.

Not only is he tall, handsome and healthy, she thought as she walked to the kitchen, *but he's so polite and well-mannered. I would dearly like to find a boy like him for my daughter.* She had taken a liking to him. She opened the fridge and took out a bottle of Coke.

"I'm afraid I've only got Coke."

"Coke would be just fine, Auntie ji."

She poured the Coke into a glass, gave it to him, and sat facing him.

"It was good to speak with Bonita the other evening. She's a nice girl, you must be really proud of her."

"Yes, she is a good daughter and I am very proud of her. She's not like some of the other girls at her university, indulging in smoking, drinking and boyfriends. Her education must not be hampered by her interests in boys or by anything. I will make sure of that. You know, lots of girls go down that road and regret it all their lives. My daughter must complete her education before thinking about boys or marriage."

Outside a succession of sharp screams, cries and raised voices could be heard followed by shouting and swearing. Apparently a small child had been knocked over by a passing motorcyclist. A group of people gathered very quickly and got hold of the motorcyclist. They gave him a good beating indiscriminately on the say-so of an elderly woman who was partially blind. No one knew what had happened. No one had seen or knew the truth except the rider as the child was too young, about three or four years of age. As far as the crowd was concerned, the rider was the guilty party. They were not interested in what he had to say. They felt he was at fault for not seeing the child stepping in front of him and that he should have swerved out of the child's way. As a result they had to teach him a lesson there and then. They were the judge and the jury. The child was taken to the nearest medical centre by a neighbor and a messenger went to inform his mother at a nearby school where she worked as a class room assistance. The rider picked himself and his machine up and limped away before further beatings were dished out by new arrivals. The crowd gradually left the scene in ones and twos and calm was restored.

"Uh-huh," said Mrs. Datta. "I know my daughter inside out and she knows her priorities. She will do as I say and, of course, she does, she has never let me down so far, and I expect nothing less of her. She is a good daughter and of course she misses her father terribly." Suddenly her eyes filled with tears.

"Don't upset yourself," Naj remarked kindly.

She seemed startled: "I am all right, really." She reached for a paper tissue from the coffee table, used it to wipe her eyes and then blew her nose into it. She looked sadly at Naj. "You must excuse me for that, it's still very painful for us."

"Of course," said Naj slowly. He glanced at his watch and noticed that he had been with Mrs. Datta for almost an hour.

"Is that the time? I must be getting back," he said, standing up. "Grandmother must be worried to death not knowing where I am."

She rose. "What's the hurry? Stay a little while longer. I'll just phone her and let her know that you're here with me. She wouldn't mind, really. In fact, I'll ask her to join us, that would be nice, don't you think?"

He moved towards the door. "Maybe another day, Auntie ji; I'll bring her with me, I promise," he said, with a smile. He could read her face, rather flushed, wanting to talk more, on and on.

"You're most welcome, just pop around any time."

She was an attractive woman, rather sweet, but lonely, he thought. He hadn't forgotten how she abused Ramu the other day, for which she had apologized, but he saw the other side of her. He felt there was a dignity in her, a solitude that he admired. She walked him to the gate at the end of the garden path and watched him leave. She kept smiling, her hand clutching the gate until he was out of sight. She slammed the gate shut and walked slowly back.

I like him, she thought. *I like him very much, he's a nice young man. It would be wonderful if I was able to find someone like him for my Bonita. All my prayers would be answered and my responsibilities over, with a son-in-law of his caliber to take care of her. I'd have nothing to worry about and my Bonita would be so happy.*

Bonita had bloomed like a wild flower over the last twelve months. Her slim figure and striking features was a magnet for boys of her age. She kept her mother restless and watchful when a group of boys with admiring eyes were present in the neighborhood. There were youths who rode their motorbikes the length of the street over and over again at night, or sat on the nearby wall in order to get Bonita's attention. One evening Bonita was passing on her way to see a girlfriend down the road when one of the boys let out a wolf whistle. She had paused for a moment and given them a stare.

"Hello, Bonita," said Rasheed with a smile in cool, trendy style, imitating a Bollywood hero actor. "How about me and you go for a ride on my motorbike?" His friends laughed. Bonita knew Rasheed lived two streets away. His sister Pinky was a year below at Bonita's Uni. Knowing her social position in the neighborhood, the retort came easily to Bonita's lips: "Does your father knows you're harassing females like me, Rasheed?" She carried on walking, majestically and gracefully. A few seconds later, another wolf whistle from the group made her stop and look back at them: "If you don't put a stop to this I'll have no choice other than to speak to your parents."

Bonita's words had an immediate impact on the youths. They all jumped off the wall, collected their motorbikes, and began walking slowly towards the shops.

Bonita met her newlywed neighbor Suresh and his wife Rosy returning from the temple's evening prayers.

"Namaskar, Bonita."

"Namaskar, bhabi ji. Namaskar Suresh bhaji," she greeted them warmly.

"Those rascals, they weren't being respectful to you, were they?" he asked.

"Oh no, no bhaji, I'm fine," Bonita confessed. She didn't want to reveal that a boy named Raju from the neighboring street had been giving her unwanted attention lately. If word ever reached Suresh, he'd be furious. There was no male figure in the Datta house and Suresh was like her own brother in the way he protected her, especially since her father passed away and her real brother moved to America.

Rosie remained quiet by his side, occasionally adjusting her patterned sari.

"Don't be afraid to let me know if they do, OK?" *They've nothing better to do with their time than to harass people going about their business, I need to have a little talk with those goon-days*, he thought.

"Yes, bhaji," said Bonita, finger-combing her hair. She couldn't help admiring Rosy's outfit, especially her sari.

Look at it, it's so beautiful, Bonita thought with a tiny twist of envy. *I'm going to dress like that and show off when I get married.*

"Bonita, hold out your hands, take parsad, here, take your share," said Rosy with a smile.

"Thank you bhabi ji, I'll save a bit for mummy ji." Bonita could tell from the way Rosy and Suresh glanced at each other that the couple was in a hurry to get away. "If you'll excuse me, I'm running late for my appointment," said Bonita and headed towards her girlfriend's house.

Is the girl psychic? Rosy wondered. She had timed her exit perfectly.

CHAPTER SEVEN

They had arrived after lunch, a little after two. It was a very hot day. The driver took two small boxes from the boot of the car and followed the three women into the house. They looked like gifts, neatly wrapped. It was so hot that Naj was taking a shower for the second time that day. After a brief visit inside, Jawali suggested that they sat out on the patio, under the shade of a neem tree, where it was cooler than inside. A slight breeze occasionally moved a petal or two on the tree but it was hot. Ramu brought out a tray of cold drinks and gave them a glass each. He didn't need telling. He knew the house rules.

"I'll organize tea and coffee now Mata ji," he said softly.

"Don't forget the methaee."

"No, Mata ji."

They were sitting at the table with their colored dupattas, handbags beside them, composed and smiling. Their eyes met his warmly and affectionately. Naj had such broad shoulders and he held himself so straight! He greeted them all with a soft smile and a "namaste".

"Come and sit next to your Grandma, beta," said Jawali, gesturing with her hand. He sat down and she began with the introductions: "This is your Auntie ji Darshano, and that is your Auntie ji Shakeena and this beautiful young lady's name is Sameena, Darsno's daughter."

Naj beamed a smile at each one, resting his elbow on the table, and they all smiled back. In the background they could hear the mellow sounds of music by Harj-D. Naj had an admirable manner, as he sat straight and confident.

How delightful to see a young man full of confidence, Darshano thought.

"It must be difficult for you, this hot weather?" asked Darshano, moistening her lips.

"Yes, it is rather hot. I don't know how one puts up with this heat, day in and day out, for months on end," replied Naj.

"April, May and June are the worst months. Sometimes it's so hot that you can't breathe."

I'm finding it hard to breathe in this heat, how would I cope in the heat of April, May and June? He thought, wiping the sweat from his brow.

"How was your trip, beta?" said Shakeena.

Naj would have been much happier if she hadn't asked him this question, she wasn't to know it had been a traumatic experience. The events of losing Sonia came flooding back. He nodded and smiled uneasily. All the same, he behaved like a gentleman. "Fine," he replied.

Jawali took a calming breath. However, she could see beyond his words; the pain, the anguish across his face, behind that thin smile.

"Ramu, hurry up with the tea," she shouted. She had the sense to improvise in such awkward, sensitive situations.

"I'll be right there, Mata ji."

The cat snoozed in the shade nearby. "Look at my Shaanti over there. Not a care in the world," said Jawali pointing. "She's no fool, she's a clever cat, much smarter than us humans." They all looked and smiled.

Dev Delay

Ramu poured the tea from the pot into each cup and placed it in front of each person. He placed the tray of methaee in the middle of the table with five small plates, spoons and a bowl of sugar.

"Do you take sugar in your tea, Auntie ji?" Naj asked Darshano, who was sitting next to his Grandmother.

"Haan beta, just a teeny bit," she replied with a smile, indicating with her forefinger and thumb. She spoke for the other two women, indicating the same amount for them. He looked over to the girl and suggested that they help themselves to the methahee. The girl hesitated at first, then took a piece of white barphee that Ramu had arranged on a tray for them.

"I can't resist methaee, even when I'm full," she said, looking across to his Grandmother.

"Have as much as you like, putter," Jawali suggested. The girl nibbled on the burphee whilst glancing over to her mother who made a face at her and then turned to Naj and smiled. It was the wrong thing to say, especially in this setting, she thought. She was not happy with her daughter behaving in that manner, her small talk embarrassed her.

Sameena thought of her mother as a domineering, hot-headed, fat old woman. *The burphee is there for eating and Jawali didn't mind me helping myself,* she thought. *Why is she making faces at me? She's just jealous of my flat tummy, my looks, my figure, that's all it is. I know it, jealous old goat. I can see her wrinkling her forehead at me when others are not looking our way.* It made no difference. Sameena didn't stop until her plate was completely clean. Even the tiniest crumbs had gone into her mouth. Her behavior lightened Naj's mood. His Grandmother was relieved. Darshano, on the other hand, was upset by her daughter's behavior.

Journey Home

They began to talk about things other than Naj's trip; about clothes, the vegetable patch, plants, flowers, Bhiaries and, of course, the cat. The atmosphere became more relaxed and Darshano and Jawali felt everything was going to be alright. A sparrow perched on the table, turned its head from side to side, helped itself to the crumbs and fluttered away leaving a mess by the tea pot. They all stared at it.

"Damn birds," said Jawali. A child cried in the distance.

"Ramu, Ramu," Jawali cried. "Come and clean this mess. Hurry up." Ramu came running with a piece of cloth and wiped away the mess.

"I've heard England is a much nicer place to live than Canada or America. I've heard there are many old and interesting buildings and a long history of kings and queens. Some day I'd like it to see it all for myself," said the girl's mother, glancing at Naj, putting the last bit of a laado into her mouth and wiping her mouth with a paper tissue, gold bangles clinking as she moved her arm and sipped the last drop of tea from the cup.

"Why not, Aunty ji? London is not that far. It only takes eight or nine hours on the plane and I'm sure Mum and Dad will put you up for a few days."

Jawali smiled at Naj. "You two young people stay here and have a chat together," she said. "While we three ladies pay a visit to the washroom." The three ladies exchanged glances. That was enough. They knew what they had to do. They all stood up. Sameena wanted to accompany them but Jawali insisted that she stayed behind and kept Naj company. Sameena looked at her mother who looked back at her and said: "You two stay here and get to know each other, we won't be long." Sameena flushed.

Dev Delay

Naj sat down, followed by Sameena. Naj didn't know what to say or do. After a moment he asked, "Would you like some water?" She nodded, but evaded his eyes. He poured water into a glass from a bottle and handed it to her. She took a sip and stared at the door constantly, silently hoping for her mother to call her to join them in the house.

Sameena was no more than eighteen. She was dressed in a traditional Panjabi suit, a salwar-kameez to match with a lightly printed purdah resting across her shoulders. She wore her carefully groomed hair down her back. Her mouth was full, her eyes big and dark, and she was beautiful, like a rose in full bloom. A slight sweat broke out on her forehead. Naj looked at her again. She simply sat there, looking shy, apprehensive and nervous, her eyes cast down and troubled. After a lingering glance at the door, she moved back into her seat.

"Would you like a biscuit?" Naj asked, trying to make conversation.

She hesitated for a second and then replied, "No, thank you." Naj insisted and moved the plate towards her. "Oh, OK then, I'll have one if you insist." She leaned forward and picked up a biscuit from the tray, her eyes fixed on the door.

"How far did you travel to get here?" he enquired, trying to keep the conversation going. She looked up, opened her mouth to speak and hesitated. Trying to help her, Naj said, "You don't need to be nervous. I'm not going to eat you or anything."

A strange smile appeared on her face and she said, "I'm not nervous!" Her exclamation disintegrated into uncontrollable giggles, and she looked at him, laughing hysterically, unable to sit still.

Journey Home

Shit, he thought, *the girl must be on drugs or something, maybe she's mad.* Suddenly she stopped and stared at her feet. Now it was Naj's turn to look towards the door, hoping for someone to rescue him from this strange, mad girl. After a few silent moments Naj asked, "Do you mind if I ask you another question?"

"No, I don't mind," she replied in a soft, low tone.

"Are you the silent type?"

"No, she mumbled. "It's—it's just that I don't know what to say to you."

"Well, OK, I'll ask you the questions and all you have to do is come up with the answers, so tell me, what do you do? I mean, are you at college or do you have a job?"

"I—I've just finished my 12th class . . ." her voice trailed away as she saw the women talking amongst themselves by the front door. She asked about his education, his ambitions and about England.

"Don't they look good together?" asked Sameena's mother as she looked towards Naj and her daughter chatting.

"They do, don't they just," Grandmother Jawali agreed.

"Ah . . . so young, so beautiful," she sighed. "It reminds me of my engagement."

"You must be joking, you were never there when your father and Uncle Saleem had you engaged to Tarlock. I remember it clearly." They all laughed as they walked over to the young couple. Sameena's mother was holding a round tray in her hands. They were about to execute their plan. Naj had no idea what they had in mind for him. He was naive about Indian culture and traditions and had no idea of the significance of what was about to happen. They

131

deposited the tray on the table and took their seats. The expressions on their faces gave nothing away.

"So what did you children talk about?" Jawali enquired, looking directly at them.

"Oh, nothing much, Grandmother, I just asked Sameena about what she did, you know?"

"Good. She's a lovely girl," Jawali said wistfully.

Naj nodded, mindful not to disappoint her. He couldn't help remembering Lucy, the first time he told her how lovely she looked when they were on their first dinner date at the Taj Mahal restaurant in the West End. Sameena was certainly very beautiful and her innocence was alluring, but there was no comparison between Sameena and Lucy, his English rose. As he watched her, he couldn't help noticing again how shy, shallow and strange she seemed.

Naj had noticed how quiet it was. The women were exchanging glances and he was puzzled. Something was not right. He wondered if he had behaved improperly with Sameena in their absence, but when he looked at her she was fine. Why were they behaving in a strange manner? It was confusing.

"Is everything all right?" he asked his Grandmother quietly. She nodded with a light smile.

Ramu came and asked if there was anything else they needed.

"Nothing, beta," Jawali told him. When Ramu left, Jawali glanced at the girl's mother, who knew what she had to do. She stood and reached for the tray, picked up a laado, broke off a small piece, and leaned over to Naj.

"Open your mouth, beta," she said with a smile. He looked across at his Grandmother in confusion.

"Take a piece from your auntie's hand, Naj dear," his Grandmother said. He looked at her, puzzled.

Journey Home

"I don't mean to be impolite or rude, but I don't have a taste for Indian sweets, I'm sorry."

The women looked at each other in confusion. His Grandmother turned to him quickly with a nervous smile: "Just take a small piece, beta. Do it for me. A small piece won't hurt you. Besides, it tastes really nice." Her voice sounded empty and hollow, as though she had suffered a great loss. He still wasn't sure and made a face, the kind a child makes when refusing to take medicine. The look on their faces said "What do we do now?" All the women relapsed into silence and stared at each other.

Unknowingly, Naj came to their rescue. He had no idea what he was getting himself into. "Alright, Aunty ji; I'll try a small piece."

Smiles appeared on the women's faces immediately. Sameena's mother placed a small piece of laado into his mouth and touched him on his head with the palm of her hand, as if she were blessing him.

"Take this little gift from me," she said as she gently squeezed a thousand rupee note into his hands before turning away. The tray of methaee was passed around. Everyone except Naj took a small piece and ate it. The ladies hugged each other in delight. Their plan was executed and they were very pleased with themselves. Naj sat and watched them, smiling, as cool as a cucumber. The perfect host, and a perfect fool. He didn't have a clue. He had no idea. He was an Anglo-Indian streetwise university graduate robbed of his dignity in broad daylight by his own flesh and blood. He did not suspect anything. Why should he? He had no reason to. After all, he was at home with his Grandmother and her old friends sitting around the table in the sunshine, chatting, drinking tea, eating sweet things and generally having a good time. What could concern him other than making it on time for a football kick-about? Who would have believed, just a week ago, that Naj would be engaged to a young, beautiful, crazy Indian girl without even realizing it? More to the point, his girlfriend Lucy, back in England, didn't have a clue either. Sameena stood, powdered her face, and smiled at him. He smiled back.

So romantic, the ladies thought.

Sameena's mother turned to Jawali with a glowing smile. "Mata ji," she said. "It's getting late and we must be getting back before dark."

There was a strange air of unreality about the whole visit. It had crossed Naj's mind to ask questions, but he had thought it was just some sort of Indian custom or a tradition. He looked at his watch. It was almost four p.m.

"Yes, of course," Jawali said. "It's not safe for us ladies to be out and about in the dark."

The visitors said their good-byes and set off. Naj changed into his football gear and ran out to take part in the football training session at the Dusshera ground. Later that evening, Naj received a call on his mobile from his mate, Tom: "Hey dude, how's it going?"

"I'm having the time of my life," he laughed.

"I wish I was there with you."

"It's just nice to be here. To be honest, mate, I hated this place initially, then suddenly, it started to grow on me. Now it just seems so real, and my Gran . . . she's just terrific, man. I can't fault her in any way. We talk all the time, just the two of us. Catching up on lost time, you know, we are just getting to know each other and I'm just generally chilling out. I'm so happy here."

"What are the women like? Just give me the juicy bits." There was excitement in Tom's voice, even though the line wasn't all that clear.

"Beautiful, just beautiful. They're nothing like English women, they are so sophisticated and graceful."

"I bet you are shagging yourself silly, me old mucker," he laughed.

"No man, don't be stupid, things are different here. It's nothing like back home, you wouldn't understand."

"What do you mean I wouldn't understand? I know everything I need to about women. They're all the same in my book, good for one thing and one thing only."

"Yeah, yeah, you clown. So tell me something that I don't know."

"What's that?"

"Why do they all leave you as soon as they find out what you're really like? Your first wife, what's her name?"

"Rose."

"Yeah, Rose, she walked out on you straight after your honeymoon and that Jackie Palmer, your second wife, she kicked you out on the street only two days after your register office wedding. Didn't you get the message? Didn't you learn anything?"

"Don't rub it in, man. Besides, there are plenty more fish in the sea, like my old boss at work used to say."

"True, brov, but you have to treat women with more respect than that. You can't treat them like a piece of meat. 'Just good for one thing', as you put it." *Will he ever change?* Naj wondered.

"It's breaking up, Naj, I can't hear you, you are breaking up." He lifted his voice. "I'll call you." Suddenly the phone went dead.

Tom, a working-class drop-out, was one of those boys who missed out on formal education. For one reason or another, he stopped going to school after his fourteenth birthday. He had no role model to look up to and no one to guide him. As for his father, he didn't see him until he went to look for him. He eventually found him when he was eighteen, and learned that he didn't want anything to do with him. As for his other experiences, he learned them all from his mates, on the street, and in various young offenders' institutions. Because of his mother's boyfriend, he had left home and moved in with an older woman. Tom struggled to adapt and the women in his life took full advantage of his good nature and vulnerability. On the whole, he considered himself a good sort, in comparison to many with similar backgrounds and experiences.

The following day, Mrs. Datta popped around as Naj was about to take a shower. "Namaste, beta," she greeted him in the living room.

"Namaste, Auntie ji."

"Kaisay ho? [How are you]"

"Fine, thank you," he replied.

She smiled at him cheerfully and enquired if Jawali was in the house.

"No," Naj said. "She's gone to the Gurdwara" He offered his visitor refreshments.

"That's very kind of you, a cup of masala chai would be nice," she said, taking a seat on the sofa.

"Are you doing anything this morning?" she asked.

"No, not really," he responded.

Ramu brewed a cup of masala tea for Mrs. Datta and got a glass of orange juice for Naj. They sat on the veranda and she took advantage of the situation. He just sat and listened.

"My daughter Bonita," she said, "is a very bright girl. She is studying for a degree in Law at the most sought-after university in the whole of Panjab."

"What university would that be?" he enquired.

Journey Home

She leaned towards him. "Oh, the one and only of course," she said. "The K. K. M. University for Women in Jalandhar. It's the elite, it is the best."

"I'm sorry; I've never heard of it," Naj commented.

"It's not widely known outside India and that's why you may have not heard of it."

"Ah, that explains it."

"You know, it's not easy to get a place in there. Many of the students are from rich families and I've heard some of them had to bribe the principal in order for their daughters to secure a place on the course." She paused to sip from the cup and continued: "It's not about how bright the child is, or the high grades they've managed to achieve; it's often about their family's status and wealth. If you've got the right resources you can buy anything in this country, anything at all." She made a face. "Does that kind of thing happen in your country too?"

"Excuse me, Auntie ji, I didn't understand," Naj said with a confused expression.

"I mean, do people in authority take bribes in the UK?"

"I'm not aware of any but I'm sure it happens there too."

There was a silence for a moment and she started again: "Let me tell you about my son Namesh. He is working in America on a two year employment visa. He was a lucky boy to get a job with a multinational company. You know, he is very good with computers. His pay is four times greater than he would earn in India. He sends most of his earnings to me each month, God bless him."

Naj sat listening. *This woman can talk*, he thought. She went on and on, in that very high-pitched voice.

"Every morning I go to the temple and pray for my children's health and wealth. I really do hope that Namesh will be allowed to stay in America permanently. As soon as he gets his green card, Bonita and I will be joining him." She shifted her gaze to the window and stretched. "I thought I saw somebody," she murmured.

"Oh, it's probably nothing," he said.

"Ah, as I was saying, I speak to him every week and each time I say to him, 'Son, you'd better hire the services of a good solicitor who could help you to get the green card'."

"So you would leave India and move to America?"

"Yeah," she said without hesitation. "I love India but America has more opportunities, don't you think, beta?"

It seemed that Mrs. Datta desperately wanted to live in the U.S.A. She was not happy with what she had. It was more than enough for a comfortable lifestyle but she craved more material things like a big house with all the latest mod cons, a heated swimming pool, a big four by four or two and all the other goodies America had to offer as the answers to her problems. Naj thought that it was a great disappointment to hear her talk like that.

"I suppose so," he said, "but I wouldn't live there myself. It's full of guns and violence. America doesn't appeal to me."

"You are serious, aren't you?" She was slightly disappointed in him for talking down America, her dream country, but thought him to be the most honest and original mind she'd ever met.

"I'm sorry you feel the U.S.A. is not for you, but my Namesh loves it there; he says people are so kind and considerate. Besides, there are good and bad people everywhere in the world." She shifted her bottom. "Even here, things are getting bad with all these Biharis coming in by the lorry-load every day." She sighed. "It's not safe to walk the streets any more, they'll cut off your hand to get at your jewelry, gold bangles and watches, anything valuable. They're not choosey. Believe me, there are lots of stories locally and throughout Panjab where people have been robbed of their goods and even killed. Just ask your Grandmother."

Does she really know all that, or is she just making it up? He wondered.

"I must admit, I do like the way American women look after themselves. I was watching a program on television the other day about a fifty-year-old woman from Seattle. She looked so beautiful and young, nothing like her real age. Then they showed another woman and she was almost sixty. She was from South India originally. She admitted to having done something to her face, but she looked fantastic too, hardly a wrinkle on her face. It was an amazing program to watch, a real eye opener."

"There are lots of Indian people living and working in America. I'm sure you'll be happy there with your two children."

"I have spoken to a relative about their daughter as a match for my Namesh. He trusts me totally to find him a good wife."

Mrs. Datta was one of those people who dreamt constantly about wealth and status. "Status is very important in our society," she told Naj. She and her husband had been bent on getting rich before he passed away with a heart attack a few months before. He had had a history of heart problems. The family had consulted some of the top doctors in Panjab and paid them thousands of rupees for their services. Nothing helped. They made large donations to God's house to no avail. Sadhus, pandits, faith healers and priests all took her money too; nothing worked. Desperate families try anything; she took each person's advice seriously and followed their instructions in detail. She had bathed in the Satluj River under the full moon; she had danced naked around the holy fire; she made parsad with her own hands and gave it to the sacred cow every Sunday for six weeks; she stood on one leg for twelve hours. She drank water from the Holy Mountain and rivers. She took potions prescribed by the sadhus and pandits. Nothing worked, but she never gave up until his last breath.

"It was fate," she said. "God had written before he was born, the date, the time for him to go back. We all tried to save his life, but there was nothing anyone could do. God had asked for his return and he went." She extracted a handkerchief from her sleeve and wiped away a tear. "I was widowed at forty-six. It's so unfair. I have two unmarried children."

She had wondered how she would cope without Ashok for the rest of her life. She knew she had to be strong for the sake of her children. She contemplated taking her life a number of times, then she thought of her children. Relatives came with their sympathy and support. She thanked them for their kind words and condolences. The time had passed painfully and the so-called relatives gradually drifted away. Since Ashok's death, her life had changed completely. She missed his company but found comfort in her two beautiful children. She had learned to support herself and, of course, the children. She understood that their lives would never be as joyful as before, because the loss of her husband affected their daily existence.

"Nothing could have prepared me for my husband's death," she said. "Losing your life partner is hard, very hard. Facing a life alone scared the hell out of me." Suddenly, her

Journey Home

eyes filled with tears and she began to weep. Naj handed her a paper tissue and she used it to wipe her eyes. She looked across at Naj. "You must excuse me for that, it's still very painful, losing Ashok so suddenly."

"Of course," said Naj slowly. Then, after a pause, "You must miss him terribly."

The empathy in Naj's words made her turn and look at him. She sighed. "When Ashok was alive," she said, "I wrapped my life around him and the children. Now it's just Bonita and me. She is almost an adult and needs me less and less except for food, clothing and money."

Suddenly a black crow came down and started picking at a piece of rubbish by the back door, breaking the momentary silence.

"See, that's a good sign," she said.

"What's a good sign?"

"The black crow, beta. It's him; I know it, it's got be him."

It seemed she had a deep interest in superstition or supernatural. "It's a well-known thing not to wash your hair on Thusday. No, it is not good." She moved her head from side to side. "Believe me, beta I know." Naj looked confused and her talking like that gave him the creeps.

"Have you ever suffered from nightmare?

"Sure. Terrible thing, nightmares, Aunti ji."

"Well, to stop it happening you sleep with a shoe under your bed, it's easy as that."

"Interesting, yeah, I'll try that if it ever happened again." Naj pulled the baseball cap lower over his face. *"This woman is truly fucked up and needs her head examining before she fucks up her daughter with all that superstitious shit."*

He felt like walking away but chose to be neighborly and smiled his false smile—"You must get lonely being on your own."

She shook her head. "No, no. I can't afford to get lonely. I'd sink very quickly if I did that." She drew a breath and straightened her back. "Now that their father has passed away I have to stay strong for my children." She paused for a second and then added, "My children need me more now than ever." She was almost in tears when Ramu walked in.

"Sir," Ramu said. "I have organized your shower and I'm off to the fish market. I'll be back as quickly as I can. Sir, do you need anything from the shops whilst I'm there?"

Mrs. Datta glanced at her watch. "Is that the time?" she said. "I have an appointment with the head masseur in about ten minutes. I'm afraid I have to leave you. Oh, and thanks for the tea and for listening to my problems." She stood up to leave as Jawali walked through the door.

"Namaste, Mata ji."

"Namaste."

"I was just leaving, woh . . . malish kernay wali aati hogi, I must go and warm the oil before she comes."

"Theek hai bhai, theek hai . . . ham sab ne jana hi hai, pehlay parsad toh lay lo."

Mrs. Datta left with parsad in her hand, saying that she'd call around later to catch up with Jawali.

Jawali sat down slowly next to Naj with the aid of her walking stick. "What did she have to say for herself today?" she enquired.

"Oh, nothing much. She told me her life story, then cried a bit and laughed a little, and then cried a bit more. She comes across as a nice person, but . . ."

"But, what?"

Journey Home

"I don't know that I should be saying this. I mean, I don't know her that well."

"Saying what, beta?"

"I mean she . . . she was very emotional at times and also I detected lots of insecurities in her actions. Mood swings . . . you know what I mean."

"Emotional?"

"Yes, Grandmother, emotional."

"There's a thing to think about, and to talk about . . . It's part of the Eastern way of life, we are culturally very emotional people."

"I didn't know that."

"It's true, we are. We Indians are very emotional people. We take everything very personally, very personally indeed."

"Yes, OK, that explains it. It's true what they say about learning something new everyday." He touched his Grandmother's arm. "Oh, before I forget, she invited us around for tea and biscuits. Her daughter will be at home too so it'll be good to meet her again."

"When did she say to go around?"

"Tomorrow evening."

"Good."

"She is a nice woman, Mrs. Datta."

"That she is."

"I felt sorry for her, widowed at only forty-six. That's so unfair."

"Yes," she sighed. "I feel sorry for her too. Being widowed at her age is the worst thing for an Indian woman. If she is seen talking openly with a man people start gossiping by putting two and two together and making five. The whole thing is usually innocent but, no, the rumors will continue to spread and spread like a wildfire, eventually destroying the poor woman's mind and soul. That's the kind of society we have to put up with." She herself had had to face such humiliating, degrading treatments at the hands of a few narrow-minded neighbors when she was widowed at the age of thirty two. "I have much sympathy for the poor woman," she sighed. She forgot about the parsad, and then it came to her. "Oh Naj, beta, your hands. Are they clean?"

Naj glanced down at the palms of his hands. "Why?"

"I want to give you parsad."

"No, Mata ji, I was about to take a shower when Auntie ji came around and I didn't get a chance to do anything."

"Now, go and get cleaned up and take parsad. Where's Ramu? Ramu come, beta, come and get your share! Maybe he's in the back garden," she muttered to herself and went to look for him.

CHAPTER EIGHT

Naj began to strike up acquaintances with neighbors, shopkeepers, taxi drivers, market traders and door-to-door peddlers. Every time he passed his shop, he greeted Sardar ji, the owner of Surinder Tailors. Sardar ji smiled back at him and extended his "namaste". On one occasion, Sardar ji called him over and the pair chatted over a cup of tea. Their relationship began to grow with each meeting and Naj enjoyed his company. During one visit they got on to the topic of the latest trends, designs and fashions. Sardar ji told Naj that in India they didn't waste time creating and inventing things. It was much easier and simpler to copy from imported goods.

"We will copy anything and everything that might make money," he said. "What is the point spending time and money creating and developing things from scratch when one can copy it from a readily available design with minimum effort? We have all sorts of tourists who come into our shops wearing or carrying something interesting. We take down the style and design and it will be available for sale the following day. Guaranteed, it's that simple."

Naj gave him an injured look, and left thinking, *it's not right stealing someone else's idea to make money. I do wish someone put stop to this sort of practice.*

Naj was a regular around the shops and the market square now. He observed, explored, and talked, as well as looking for interesting items to take back for his friends and parents as gifts. He quickly learned the art of haggling from observing Ramu at work with the traders, but he was still a novice and ignorant in many ways. One day he walked into an arts and decor shop in the market place. As he was looking at a painting that caught his eye, he thought it would make a good present for his Mum and Dad. He asked the old storekeeper about the two people in the painting, represented as holding a round clay pot. The shop owner looked astonished at his ignorance. "That's Sohani and Mahiwal," he said, scratching his bald head. Leaving the store, Naj felt embarrassed. He had no notion who Sohani and Mahiwal were and didn't particularly care, but he liked the painting.

"How am I supposed to know about Indian folklore?" he muttered to himself. "I'm an Englishman, not an Indian for God's sake!" *I'll ask Ramu,* he thought, *perhaps he'll be able to enlighten me on the matter; he must know.*

One morning Naj was taking a stroll in the neighborhood when he noticed a group of about twenty women in colored saris with loose hair hanging down their backs running towards a neem tree by the roadside. On reaching the tree they sat and listened to their leader, chanting religious hymns. Suddenly, they all stood up after their leader and began stamping the earth beneath their feet, chanting, groaning and gasping. This went on for four to five minutes. Then they bent down on all fours and began thumping the ground with the palms of their hands and spinning their heads round and round. This went on for half an hour. They had brought pots, pans and food items which they cooked on an open fire. A small offering was made to an ant mound before they shared the food amongst themselves. They got up and walked back towards the place they had

Journey Home

came from and soon disappeared out of sight. Naj stood scratching his head, wondering what they were doing. He went home, told Jawali and asked her to explain.

"It is a religious thing, beta," she said. "They worship Devi through a medium. Then the spirit of Devi enters one of the women. They communicate through her and answers are provided to their individual problems and their deceased are contacted."

Naj was fascinated by this, but his curiosity prompted him to ask another question: "Is it a sort of witchcraft?"

"No," she said. "No, beta, not witchcraft." Suddenly, Jawali grew pale. Naj had to put his arm about her. He felt there was more to it than his Grandmother had told him, at least in theory. Wisely, he did not press her further on the issue, not wanting to upset her. Naj's parents had often told him how wonderful and enjoyable a trip to India would be. He would have preferred a trip to Thailand, like so many of his friends, rather than going to India. Now he had only been here a short period, just over two weeks, and he had started to see India in a different light. His experience to date had already impacted on his thoughts about life. After all, India was his ancestral home and he had begun to put the pieces together. For the first time in his life he felt how rich life was and appreciated how things were. He was gradually falling in love with his ancestral home and the Indian people. The arts, culture, tradition and faith: everything started to make sense to him. He realized that everything had meaning and purpose; he had seen it with his own eyes. He had seen both sides of the spectrum, the very rich and the very poor and their struggles in coping with almost next to nothing in material, financial terms. Some fed and clothed their families on as little as 50p a day, the rickshaw man's daily income. It had been a real eye opener for him, a real education, and he had picked up one or two survival skills. One could not conceive of the reality of life in India from pictures in books, magazines or on TV. One had to be here in the flesh in order to experience and appreciate its culture, traditions, arts, architecture, food and the reality of chaos and human existence. Regardless of Naj's initial experiences and viewpoint, India had grown on him with every moment, every breath. He had been up at the break of dawn every morning. Like the locals, he took a cold shower before his morning prayers. His diet had also changed. He preferred traditional home cooking to roadside takeaways. Roti with dhals, sabjee and paraothas were his favorites now, instead of greasy fish and chips or High Street takeaways. He had taken up yoga and meditation for a healthy mind and body. He enjoyed reading the Indian local and national news papers and listening to the news on the radio, keen to learn about its political system. His visit to the Golden Temple in Amritsar gave him in-depth pleasure and education and a platform to build his appreciation and knowledge on. Naj had read about the British Empire and its impact on India, Pakistan and Bangladesh. He'd read about the Jullianwala Bagh 1919 atrocities. Each day was full of joy and new experiences. He had made many friends amongst the local community, especially the children. He had got to know his neighbors, the shopkeepers, the sabjee man, the holy man, the sacred cow, the doodhwala, the rubbish collectors and the postman, the fortune teller, the snake charmer, and the abandoned cow. This was the sort of magical experience that money can't buy. He appreciated spending quality time with his Grandmother; eating and chatting together with her was just wonderful. He looked forward to the early morning sounds of religious prayers aired on the local radio station and through the loudspeakers mounted on roofs. He gained pleasure and confidence in knowing that people of different faiths lived peacefully, side by side. His Grandmother had seen the change in him in more ways than one. Naj had picked up words of Panjabi and had managed simple conversations with children, adults, and strangers. His love of Indian music had grown to equal his love of rock. He had started to watch Bollywood Hindi films and had listened to traditional Panjabi folk songs and dhol beats. His appetite for new experiences had grown with his appreciation of his heritage. For the first time, he had had the magical experience of sleeping under the moon and stars. He had swum in the waters of the Satluj river; milked a goat, a cow and a water buffalo. This had been a turning point of his life. His life had changed direction. He had gone to India by chance. He hadn't been looking for answers, but ended up finding them.

*

My Country

My country is my home. My thoughts confirm this. Thoughts have the right of possession. Therefore, this country of mine is owned by me and those who share my thoughts.

A sense of belonging comes from within. I belong to my country. It's here that the peacock dances under the blue sky and birds entertain me every morning with their sweet songs. And it's here the night skies glow with moonlight and stars. They watch over me as I dream in my sleep of my country.

Invaders and rulers alike have left their mark on my country and foreign influences still linger in spite of strong cultural identity, heritage, and religion. The old traditions are gradually changing. Changes are happening apace. Progress is the word on people's lips and some voices cry with sadness . . .

My country is a power and this power has given birth to many remarkable, brave individuals. Schoolchildren are taught about their place in history.

Last night I stood on one leg in a yoga pose, looked up to the sky and remembered my forefathers for their courage and their wisdom. Their gift that makes me proud of my people and my country.

I'm going to take Grandmother to Amritsar. We'll visit the Golden Temple and the Jullianwala Bagh. She'll love that. Even though she's getting on a bit in years, she'll manage it; she's a tough chapatti.

It was all arranged. The following morning, they left early in the family's car. It was a clear, pleasant day. They stopped on the way for a cold drink and petrol. By nine o'clock they had arrived at Amritsar.

Naj and Jawali enjoyed one another's company as they explored the city of Amritsar. First, they paid homage at the Sikh religious shrine, the Golden Temple. They parked close by and the driver waited in the car while the two of them headed for the temple. Jawali climbed out of the car slowly, covered her head with a dupatta and gripped tightly to her walking stick. They started to walk up the narrow path. The old lady hadn't been to Amritsar for twenty years, although she had seen the old city a number of times before and had paid her respects at the temple each time. She was just as excited about this trip as Naj. This was a special day for both of them. There was the hustle and bustle of the city and people rushing by, the noise, the smell, but she didn't mind that. They were heading towards the shrine. She felt different. With God on her mind, she felt calm and content. Halfway up the path, she stopped and straightened up.

"That is the house of God," Jawali said, pointing to the temple. "Every living soul should have the chance to come and see this unique creation of God at least once in their lifetime." Naj looked at her. "It's a pilgrimage for all Sikhs and for others who believe in justice, fairness and equality. Did you know the Sikh religion is based on equality?"

"No, I didn't know that."

"Well, now you know, beta."

Outside in the communal compound they removed their shoes and washed their feet, hands and faces and covered their heads. They walked up the steps and entered the temple through the main entrance gate. There it was in front of them. It was the most magnificent, glittering piece of architecture Naj had ever laid his eyes on. He stood in amazement as his jaw dropped. He'd seen beautiful buildings before, but nothing like this. He was overwhelmed by the sheer size of it; it took his breath away. He turned and faced the holy house, put his hands to his face, bent forward, and paid his respects. As they viewed the splendors of the dome, its gold glittered in the water below, as if it were welcoming each and everyone. He looked around. There were hundreds, if not thousands, going about peacefully observing, enjoying their pilgrimage, paying respect, connecting with God. The pull of the shrine was so powerful. He felt moved, tranquil and spiritual, all at the same time. He was so happy that he'd had the chance to see it for himself in the company of his Grandmother.

"I'll like to bring my wife and children here one day," said Naj.

She smiled. She felt happy. "That is very thoughtful of you, putter, you should do that." She paused to adjust her dupatta. "Nowhere else in the world could be more fitting for believers of Sikhism than this auspicious place of worship. Who could argue this is not a blessed place? Just feel the vibes."

Naj was totally at peace with himself as if the experience was the most natural thing in the world. Inspired to learn more he asked about the significance of the Sikh holy book. "The 'Guru Granth Shaib' is to Sikhs what the Bible is to Christians or the Koran is to Muslims and Geeta is to Hindus,"she said, with a great pride."The Guru Granth Sahib is woken up at the dawn, usually around five a.m. and put to sleep at the end of the day, after the Guru Ghar's business is completed. See, the Sikh Guru Ghar has four entrances; one facing the east, one facing the west, one facing the north and another to the south. Accessible to all from every direction. Is it not a wonderful idea?"

He nodded, trusting her completely. He was coming to recognize and appreciate that all this was good for humanity and meant to be; an open house to all, wonderful. *Why didn't my parents bring me here?* Naj thought. *This alone was worth the trip.*

The talk drifted to the 1984 attack on Harmander Sahib by the Indian army, ordered by the late Indira Ghandi, then Prime minister of India. She paid the price for it with her life soon after, when she was assassinated by her own Sikh body guards, and there were consequences for Sikhs across India thereafter. This topic was equally absorbing for Naj, and after thirty minutes or so they rose, straightened their clothes and walked off towards the buildings where the restorations were still taking place. Jawali raised her eyes at the men working away and sighed deeply. "Why . . . oh why? Attack on the shrine? Why? Attack the house of God. Was it necessary?"

They said prayers for loved ones and for world peace and ate guru ka langar at the temple with hundreds of other visitors and worshipers.

"Heaven knows when we will have another opportunity like this one," Jawali wondered. Before walking up the steps to leave Naj glanced back. The Harmander Shaib was truly a place of God, he thought.

Later in the afternoon, the driver took them to the Jullianwala Bagh. They walked up to the well and tears came to her eyes as she told him about the killings, the carnage that had taken place at the hands of the British rulers in 1919. They spent an hour or so walking in the gardens, looking at the old buildings where the bullet holes were visible in the brickwork before going down to the market for a cup of tea. Naj bought some items for Lucy from the gift shops, and then they set out to view the old architecture, the ancient ruins.

Naj had found the experience and the knowledge gained very rewarding. But the trip had been long and tiring, especially for Jawali, and on the way back she didn't say much. They drove at a steady pace. The road was busy as always. The sun had gone down and darkness descended. Naj instructed the driver to drive slowly so that they could get home safely. The locals drove like mad. Some came at you until the last second before twisting out of the way. Others drove without lights, making it difficult to see them in the dark. The driver was experienced but his eyes remained glued to the windscreen, twisting, turning, overtaking cycles, mopeds, rickshaws, buses and ox-driven carts. By the time they got home in the cool of the evening Jawali was exhausted. She soothed herself with a glass of warm milk as she had since childhood, be it a cold winter's day or a hot summer's night. Naj went straight into the kitchen and helped himself to a cold can of cola, spreading himself out on the sofa.

The night temperature had risen a degree or two higher than usual and the mosquitoes came out to feast in their hundreds. Naj didn't sleep well, tossing and turning with mosquitoes singing in his ears over and over again to the tune of Robbie Williams: *"Let me entertain you/ We're going to have a party tonight/We've been waiting for you—for a long time/ You Anglo Indian dude/ Don't look so confused/ We're going to have a party tonight/ We're going to have a party tonight with you.*" Naj was soaked in sweat and his throat was dry. He slipped out of the netted bed and went to the kitchen. He poured himself a glass of water and returned straight to bed. It took him no more than a minute or two, but within that time a squadron of mosquitoes had attacked him with military precision. He had been bitten all over and he spent the rest of the night scratching.

The following day, Jawali accidentally fell over her cat and ended up on the floor in agony. Her screams brought Ramu running from the garden. They put her in the car and she was admitted to the Cantt Military Hospital nearby. After a full examination and x-rays, the doctor revealed the result of his prognosis. "The old lady has fractured her hip," he told Naj. "She'll have to stay in hospital for some time."

Naj arranged to cover the cost, including a private room, meals of her choice and a nurse to watch over her around the clock. The doctor told him she was in good hands and promised to give her the best care possible. Jawali was operated on the following day and it all went very well. He was very positive about her recovery.

"She is a strong woman, your Grandmother," the surgeon said. "There is nothing wrong with her other than the fracture. We have examined her thoroughly and I was surprised with the results. Her blood pressure is normal, her heart is fine."

A week later, the old lady sat up in her hospital bed staring out the window. Her pale eyes were wide open. She was in a world of her own, but her eyes wouldn't focus easily. A minute went by, and then the ghost of a smile appeared on her face, as if a thought was amusing her. "Shan mare kisan ko, kisan mare app ko," Jawali commented to no one in particular.

"What did you say, Grandmother?"

"Oh nothing beta." Then: "Ha, I don't think I'll ever walk again. I'm too old . . . too old for my fractured hip to mend."

Her self-esteem was low for once and thoughts of death entered her mind. It was a sad, depressing time, but her belief in God remained at full strength.

"If God has his way, he might be tempted to take me to heaven and the reunion with your Granddad might be sooner rather than later." She slowly turned and looked at him.

Naj was immensely silent. He moved forward in his chair and looked at her, but she began to cough and splutter. "Would you like some water?" he asked. She continued coughing. He poured out a small glass and put it to her lips. She managed to take a small sip and her coughing ceased for a moment.

"How is my little baby Shaanti?" she enquired.

"Oh she's fine, just fine," he said quietly. He dared not tell her that her cat had a new home now. He was so angry with the cat he got Ramu to give it away to his cousin, who lived close by in Indira Colony.

"Make sure she is fed properly. She is very fussy about her food. She likes her fish cooked slowly. If it's not cooked to her taste, she won't eat it. Ramu knows what to do."

"Don't worry yourself, Grandmother. I'll take good care of her, I promise." *I can't tell her about the cat,* he thought. *She'll never speak to me again.*

"Thank you, beta, I know you will." Her cat meant everything to her, she could do no wrong, ever. She'd tell everyone who cared to listen that, "She didn't mean to trip me up. It was just an accident," she'd say.

A cheerful young nurse with long black hair and a slim figure made her rounds twice a day, in the morning and then in the afternoon. She checked Jawali's blood pressure, heartbeat, and made sure the drip above her bed was correct. This took her more than five minutes and then she left to attend other patients. In order to be sociable, Naj once asked the nurse about the drip bag and she went into lengthy detail about its purpose, the benefits for the patient and the man behind its invention. She soon lost him; her words were gobbledegook. After that, Naj avoided her like a plague. Her assistant, an older nurse, sat outside the room to help the old lady with her personal needs. She was there from seven in the morning until seven at night and then she was replaced by another until the next morning.

There is something demeaning about being in a nightie in the daylight. The nurses and doctors prodded the old lady's body and stuck needles into her. The whole environment of the hospital infuriated Jawali. She couldn't wait to leave the place and wanted to be with her beloved Shaanti and, of course, Ramu. She was dependent on him, not only for chores around the house, but for his unconditional warm smile, and his love. He was her lifeline and she had grown used to his loyalty and commitment. He had a knack for guessing her mind, even before she opened her mouth.

Naj plumped the pillows and helped her to lean back as she closed her eyes. It meant a lot to him to make her comfortable. Then he sat with a cup of tea in the hospital cafe thinking about his Grandmother. She had always been so independent, so energetic, so very much her own person all her life. She was ninety plus and he feared the worst, following this nasty fall. He began to feel nervous and anxious and thought about what he should do. *I'll go to the temple and pray for her first thing tomorrow.* Then his thoughts turned to the cat. *I've always hated cats and it was the cat that put my grandmother in hospital. I'm glad to see the back of it. If she enquires about it when she returns home I'll just tell her she's run away or something*, he thought.

It was a good half hour before Naj returned to her bedside. She was sitting up, feeling slightly better. "There you are. I thought you had abandoned me for good," she said with an awkward smile. "Come and sit down beside me. I want to tell you something very important." She put her hand on his shoulder and told him to pay attention. They had the room to themselves. "There's a trunk under my bed at home and inside, right at the bottom, you'll find a small box wrapped in a yellow cloth. I'll give you the keys to open it. Inside there are some old silver rupees and your Granddad's war medals. Amongst them there is one very special medal. I believe it's called the Victoria Cross. It was given to your Granddad by Queen Victoria herself for an act of bravery. It's a very important award. It is yours. I want you to have it, beta," she said with a squeeze of his hand. "Your Granddad, I'm sure, is looking down at the two of us right now, and feeling very proud of the passing of his medal to his one and only heir." Jawali liked the sense of handing on the past, be it silver rupees, items of furniture or traditions. It was a great thing to do, great indeed. *It'll keep memories alive,* she thought.

Naj's mind had wandered to the coach crash. Indeed, his own life was a miracle, he was lucky to be alive, there was no mistake about it; here he was, in the prime of his life, in the land of his forefathers. Yet the crash had almost ended his journey, right there. It nearly robbed him of this chance of being with his Grandmother. He was so happy, so very happy that he had survived.

The next day, before going to the hospital, Naj went to the temple and prayed for Jawali to get better. The sound of the temple bell gave him comfort. He returned to the hospital to be with her, holding a bunch of flowers. She was sitting waiting for him with her hands clasped. She had forgotten to wear her dentures. He laughed at the sight of her and she smiled good-humouredly back, without realizing why he was laughing.

"They're lovely," she said, touching the flowers with her hand. "Put them in water for me, dear. Are they from our garden?"

"Yes, Grandma." She was happy to know the flowers came from her garden. He held her hand as they talked, discussed neighbors, the cat, and the garden. The two of them spent the whole afternoon in each other's company, joking and laughing. She was much more comfortable. Later, she sank down in her bed, exhausted. He was pleased that she had eaten her breakfast and lunch and was looking forward to her dinner of dhal, roti and a tub of her favorite mango pickle. It pleased him to know that she was on the mend. Outside, the light was fading fast, the sun dropping, a great red, frost-rimmed ball. The birds had retired for the day. Shift workers were also returning home to their families. Before he left her bedside, she made him promise that he would bring a photograph of her cat, Shaanti, on his next visit.

On the morning of Wednesday, March 28th, Naj received a phone call from his Grandmother. She told him she was feeling rather cold and that he should bring a blanket. By the time Naj had reached her side, she was shivering uncontrollably. Dr Sodi had looked in on her and his diagnosis indicated that she had a chill. He advised her to stay in bed with extra clothing to keep warm and to take two Paracetamol every two hours. That evening, Jawali's temperature rose to 105, and by next morning 107. The cheerful young nurse had lost her cheerfulness. She feared for her elderly patient. Naj was worried sick too. Jawali taking a turn for the worse had been completely unexpected. Instead of going home on Friday, Jawali spent the following two days hooked up to antibiotics via a vein in her arm. The bottles of antibiotics dangled from a stand by her bed. Her immune system was considered weak and a risk to her well-being. Dr Sodi had advised against returning home until she was fully fit. By Saturday, her fever abated and she was feeling cheerful. By now she had enough of disinfection, needles, and nurses and wanted to go home. *If I stay here longer than necessary, I might never leave this place alive,* she thought. She, not a doctor, decided when she would leave. The next day the stubborn old lady discharged herself. Naturally, she knew Naj would be concerned, but there was no stopping her. Jawali never got to know other patients. She had spent all her time in bed, isolated in her private room. Aside from Naj and the young nurse, she had had very little company. He had visited her every day. She also had other visitors, Mrs. Datta and her friend Sabanna from Adampur. They came when she was all drugged up and she could hardly remember their having been there.

Ramu was enjoying a game of cards with his alcoholic cousin at home when he heard a car pull up outside the gate; Jawali was being helped out of the back seat by the driver. It was a hot day and Ramu had consumed over two bottles of Kingfisher. "It can't be? No. I must be seeing things. Mata ji is in hospital." He put the cards down on the small wooden table. His cousin helped himself to another bottle of beer, his fifth. Ramu rushed to the gate tying the string of his shorts. "Mata ji, Mata ji I'm coming."

Jawali, who had just remarked how well she was feeling, suddenly found herself unable to stand up or walk, even with the aid of the walking frame. She almost lost her footing and stumbled. "Goodness me," she gasped as she gripped the driver's arm. She needed to sit down before risking falling down. The driver growled words of encouragement to her. "Lean on me, dear; I've got you. I won't let you fall." Ramu rushed indoors and returned with a chair. "Here Mata ji, sit on this for a minute. Jawali sat gasping under the shade of the neem tree, making desperate attempts to regain her strength." Nothing to worry about; just give me a minute and I'll be on my feet."

Ramu rushed into the kitchen and came back with a glass of water. "Drink this, Mata ji" said Ramu putting the glass to her lips.

Jawali refused the offer of assistance, and seized the glass from his hand. "Give it here and stop being a fool," she snapped. "I can manage." She took a sip as Ramu stood by her side.

The driver was eager to be paid and had a word in Ramu's ear but was told to wait for Naj's return. But he was in a hurry and pestered to be paid so he could go about his business. Luckily Ramu had access to his savings and paid the man then told him to leave.

"Naj, where is he?" she asked softly.

"He's gone to the market. I'm expecting him home any minute," said Ramu reassuringly. Naj was at a phone shop bargaining with the salesman for a phone for Lucy when he got the call.

"Oh, Vahe Guru? . . . oh, no . . . oh, Vahe Guru . . ."

"What's the matter, Mata ji?"

"The pain . . . oh."

"Where?"

"My back, dear."

"Do you want me to send for the doctor, Mata ji?"

"Don't be silly, dear. Besides, what can he do for me other than suggesting I should take an extra tablet."

Having rested for a few minutes Jawali took a big gulp of air into her lungs and began feeling much better and gazed around at her flower beds rapturously; it was surely the best medicine for her and of course seeing Naj enter through the gates as well.

"Hello Grandmother. What's going on? Naj snapped. "What are you doing at home? Shouldn't you be in hospital?"

"Hello, beta," she replied.

"Really, Grandmother, I sometimes wonder if you know what you are doing. You do the most stupid things."

"Oh, rubbish, beta. You do *fuss.*"

"I *fuss* do I?"

"Yes you do. I'm not surprised, you're Grandfather was the same, ordering me around, making *fuss* unnecessarily over nothing."

"Over nothing? The trouble with you, Grandmother is you are too stubborn," said Naj critically. "You don't listen to advice given by those who know what is best for you. But no, you have to decide for yourself regardless."

'Yes; well, I don't see why I should have to stay there cooped up like a chicken all by myself when I'm perfectly fine.'

"So tell me, Grandmother, why would Dr Sodi suggested you should stay in hospital for another week?"

"Money, of course. What else? Another week, another bundle of rupees in his deep pockets; that's why. I got to know how his brain works when it comes to money. He pretends to be an expert on practically everything you care to mention. It's true he did a good job on me but I heard stories of horrific butchery and extortionate charges made whilst I was in there."

There was a long silence while Naj thought what to do. He decided to send for Dr.Sodi, who arrived within the hour. He checked her blood pressure and pulse, it was normal, then agreed for her to stay at home.

Jawali had been looking forward to being reunited with her beloved cat. "Where is Shaanti? She demanded. Naj and Ramu glared at each other, shocked. Ramu panicked and lied. "She's here somewhere, Mata ji. It's not long since I saw here chasing after a mouse. I'm sure she'll turn up as soon as she senses your arrival."

"Come, on baby; come to mummy." The cat was half a mile away with Ramu's cousin expecting a litter within a week to ten days according to Ramu's sister-in-law, Geeta.

Naj and Ramu helped Jawali into her bed and she told Ramu to bring her a cup of tea. "I've got the most splitting headache," she said looking sorry for herself.

"Shaanti, I wonder where she is?"

Naj and Ramu, stunned, stood in awkward silence looking at each other. Jawali closed her eyes and gently massaged her temple. Naj took Ramu to one side. Ramu didn't need telling, he knew what to do. Half an hour later Jawali and the cat were reunited. A week later Shaanti gave birth to three kittens which delighted Jawali but horrified Naj.

Jawali gradually got healthier and began to walk better with the aid of a stick. Naj was surprised to see how much better she was. He was also overjoyed to think that he would be able to return to Lucy very soon. He was seldom far from his Grandmother, as if his love for the old lady was growing by the minute. For now, she was his priority. He felt guilty. She had always been alone in that big house and now that she was old and infirm he felt she needed to be near her family. *Perhaps I could stay with her a little longer,* he thought, *and then Mum and Dad could come to stay with her for a while.* Naj shivered when he thought about what his Grandmother had told him about other old folks living alone and isolated with no one to care for them. Their sons, daughters, nieces, nephews; all of them moved abroad to America, Canada, Greece, the U.K, Holland, Germany, New Zealand and France. The old people were left to fend for themselves. *Everyone is chasing money these days, the old folks are not their priority any more, it's sad.* Naj was sure about his priorities. His conscience was clear as far as his Grandmother's situation was concerned. He would make sure that she was with her family for the remaining days of her life.

Lucy rang Naj. The two of them had hit it off from the minute their eyes first met. They got on really well. He was very comfortable in her presence and had begun to trust her. He told her of the things that he was unable to share with anyone, his innermost feelings. They had begun to spend more time in each other's company and did almost everything together; cinema, theatre, eating out, falling out and making up. Their relationship became stronger and it was obvious to them both that it was developing into something more. Three years had passed quickly. It seemed that their relationship was made in heaven. Naj had written poems about her and she gave him love letters. He had told her about his parents' strong views on mixed marriages and both of them had agreed to keep their relationship secret, at least for the time being. Naj had promised her that he'd work on his mother first and then get her to talk to his Dad. He was sure that, in time, both of them would come round to accepting the relationship. Naj had already met Lucy's mother and the two of them had spent weekends at her home in Cornwall. Lucy had travelled to India before with her girlfriend Jane and loved everything except poverty. She had a good understanding of Indian culture and often fantasized about marrying an Indian. In Naj, she saw the Indian prince of her imagination: a tall, dark, handsome, intelligent, loving person.

Naj spent the next thirty minutes talking to Lucy on the phone. He told her about his Grandmother's fall. She listened to his description of the fracture and how she ended up in hospital.

"I can't just leave her in this state," he said. "She's not a well woman. She needs me here to look after her. There's no one else and I feel it's my duty to look after her. Besides, I want to. For God's sake, can't you understand that?"

"I understand what you are saying, but what about me? I have needs too. What am I supposed to do; wait for you to return while life passes me by?" She made her case.

Sunlight played across his face as he sat on the patio talking to her. "All right, all right, tell you what I'll do,

Journey Home

I'll catch the next flight home as soon as she starts to walk again, and that's a promise."

That could be weeks away or even a month. She had heard stories from other people, about other relationships similar to theirs, where British Asian guys had gone to their parents' home for a holiday or to a cousin's wedding and returned having got engaged or married themselves. Lucy felt confused, lonely and vulnerable. "You still love me, don't you?" she asked.

"Of course I love you. You know you're the sweetest thing in my life. Why do you doubt me? Of course I love you, you stupid girl. How often do I have to say it? I love you, I love you, I love you . . ."

"I don't want to lose you, babe," she said.

"What are you talking about? Of course you're not going to lose me. I'll promise we'll make it work." Naj thought about the challenges ahead. He knew how much he loved her. There was no question about him ever wanting to hurt her, no more than he would hurt himself. He knew that what they had for each other was so powerful.

Lucy felt deeply troubled by the insecurity of being left behind, alone, but she was reassured by what he had told her. It seemed unlikely that he would abandon her now. He was a wonderful man. Every time he looked into her eyes she floated on clouds. Life without him wasn't worth living. Naj was the best thing that had happened to her, but for some reason she felt unsure and vulnerable, at least for the moment. She decided to change the subject back to his Grandmother. "So what did the doctor tell you?" she asked.

"Tell me about what?"

Lucy felt he was deliberately avoiding her question and noted tension in his voice. She rephrased her question.

165

"When do you think your Grandmother will be able to walk again? Days, weeks, when?" Lucy's voice tightened as she pressured Naj for more information.

"Soon, I hope. It could be days or it could be a week. That's what the doctor told me."

There was silence from Lucy's end of the line, as if something had happened. Naj anxiously waited for another question. He held the phone to his ear. *I told her the truth*, he thought. He had no reason to lie, but he'd feel better if Lucy was a bit more understanding and sympathetic. The shadow under the banana tree shifted towards the table. "Hello, Lucy, are you there?"

"Yes, sorry, OK, are you sure it'll be no more than a week?" Lucy said, after thinking it through.

"Sure as I can be, babe. I've told you what the doctor told me. I just can't understand why you are doubting me."

"Naj, please don't think I'm giving you a hard time for the sake of it, but I'm really missing you."

"I know you are. There is nothing to worry about, everything going to be all right, I promise. Now listen, I've got to go, I'll phone you in a couple of days. Let's hope she's on the mend by then."

Lucy felt alone and vulnerable. Naj sounded far away. She felt confused by his explanation and wanted to argue further, but half of her held her back. The last thing she wanted was to drive him away when her goal was to have him back in her arms.

"I love you too, babe," Naj said. "Bye for now. I'll phone you."

"Bye Naj, bye darling," said Lucy reluctantly. Lucy stood with the phone in her hand and couldn't help wondering what lay ahead. *Something is not right. There is something he's hiding from me, I feel it in my waters. I'm not letting go of him, no way. I've invested too much in this relationship. Nobody is going to take him away from me. He's mine and I will hold onto the most precious thing in my life, even if it kills me. If he doesn't return like he says he will, I'll go to India myself and bring him back.* She was serious.

*

Naj made his decision easily. He'd stay and look after his Grandmother for as long as it took, regardless of Lucy's pleading for him to return. He needed to release some of his grief and tension. He had to talk with his Grandmother; he had to rid himself of the awful, constant stress that was making his life a misery. He felt anxious and run down. It wasn't healthy for him to hold it in, he thought. That afternoon, he couldn't stop thinking about it. He knew he couldn't put off asking her any longer. He felt haunted and couldn't run away from it, it was time now. He picked the moment. He had made up his mind, but at the same time his throat dried and he couldn't speak. He stood up, then sat down again, hesitating. Thinking about how she'd planned the whole thing made his blood boil.

"Come and sit down, Grandmother," he said nervously. "I need to speak with you about something."

"It sounds serious, beta, but let's eat first," she said, with a wave of her hand.

"No. I'm not hungry," said Naj abruptly.

"You have to eat, putter, you'll grow thin if you start skipping your meals and we can't have that, can we?"

"What's wrong with being thin? What about your favouite actress; what's her name? Oh, it's coming to me now, that Karina Kapoor." He was deliberately being obtuse and cold.

I know something is very wrong, she thought. *Why is he not sharing with me; why is he in such denial about it?* "People will talk, they'll say Naj has lost weight because his Grandmother is not feeding him enough."

"Let them talk," he said angrily. "I don't care about what they say. Besides, it's none of their business whether I eat or not." Something was troubling him, but she was afraid to question him. Words from Naj's last conversation with Tom kept running through his mind: *Engagement, Sameena, engagement party, engagement, ladoo payrhay, engagement, Naj.* A sense of unease remained deep in his heart, mixed with troubling questions. "I have to tell you there is something troubling me. It is this; my friend Tom phoned me from England and he told me that Mum and Dad had celebrated my engagement party with that girl Sameena who was here the other day. At first, I thought he was having a laugh with me like he normally does, but he was serious. He told me that he went to the party. Everyone there was very shocked and surprised that I'd got engaged to a total stranger within days of arriving in India. I did not believe him at first, but he swore it was true. So tell me; what's going on?"

She just looked at him.

"Am I going insane or something?"

She sighed, she scratched her cheek. "Very well," she said. "I'm old enough to know that the time has come for my grandson to get married and settle down. That is what is expected of you. You are coming up to twenty-five years of age. So far as I am concerned," she continued firmly, "you've reached that stage in your life where you have to take responsibility for the family."

"I am well aware of my age. So what? That's not old by any means. I'm just a boy. I need to have fun and enjoy my youth before I settle down with a wife and kids. Besides, I'll decide when it's time for me to get married, not you and not Mum or Dad, for that matter." There was a sharp edge to his voice. He continued: "It's *my* life and I aim to live it *my* way; do you understand, Grandmother?" A dead silence filled the room.

"Naj, putter, the family's opinion comes before your own. That's how things are. Like it or not, you are going to get married, if not now then tomorrow," she said forcefully.

Dumbfounded, Naj stared at his Grandmother after this outrageous proposition. With an effort, he controlled himself. The expression in her eyes made him wonder if she really was his honest, kind, caring Grandmother. He felt angry and confused. Silence fell once more.

Shall I break the news? He thought. *Shall I tell her I have a girlfriend in England and that I'm already engaged to her? If I tell her the truth, how will she take it, what will she do? It may be too much for her heart and I can't afford to take that chance.*

"It isn't any good playing silly games with me, is it? Sooner or later I would have found out and, besides, how on earth would you have married me off without me knowing about it?"

She made no reply. After a moment, Jawali said, "I'm sorry, putter, I didn't mean to hurt you. I'm so, so sorry you feel this way. Look at it from the plus side: Sameena is perfect for you. She is known to the family and she is blessed with purity and sweetness. What more could a boy like you want in a girl? She is obedient and delicate, a little shy perhaps, but very pretty with it. She'll make you a good wife."

Naj sat staring at Jawali. He frowned.

"Grandmother, please listen to what I say. I'm not ready for marriage, OK? Not at the moment. The girl is all of those things; she is incredibly beautiful and lovely. I'm sure she'll make someone a good wife, but she is not for me."

Jawali sat remorsefully under his gaze, but she held herself upright. She was disappointed that he had rejected Sameena.

Naj raised his brows. "What are you going to do now, Grandmother?"

She sat in silence, thinking. She adjusted her scarf. Her thoughts raced. Jawali sensed how sad and upset he had become. She was worried about his well-being. She had thought and thought about it deeply, but somehow she couldn't bring herself to object any longer. What right did she have to deprive him of his happiness?

He'll come around to the idea of marriage in a year or two, she thought, *and when he does I will be the first to help him find the girl of his choice.*

"Naj, look at me," she said. "Darling, it's not too late, you know." He did not look at her. There was no sign that he had heard a single word.

"Naj beta," she continued. "We did it for your own good and for the good of this family. All you have to do is say you do not want this girl and I'll understand. No one will blame you for changing your mind. Nobody is going to think any less of you or that you are a bad boy. After all, you are allowed to reject a few girls before you decide on the one you think will be a good wife. There are so many other educated, beautiful girls waiting in the queue for you to choose from. I'll phone Meetoe, the go-between lady; she'll arrange it for us."

"Grandmother, stop it. Please, stop." Naj interrupted. "You are being ridiculous now."

The anger in his voice disturbed her. Suddenly it went quiet in the room. It was so silent that one could have heard a pin drop. He held his head in his hands and stared at the floor for a moment.

"Grandmother, listen to me. I'm not a child. I have lived a little, although not as much as yourself. I have a university degree. I have learned to respect other people's point of view and I believe that one mustn't try to live another's life for them. I know the difference between right and wrong. It is my life, my future, my happiness that you are talking about and not your damn cat's, all right?"

"Come, come, my child. You don't have to worry about any of this. Your Grandmother will fix it."

"Fix what? You have already fixed it for me, haven't you, Grandmother? Why don't you just put a rope around my neck and fix it for me forever?"

"Chheeh! Chheeh! There's no need to talk like that, putter. Please don't upset yourself over this. It's not your fault, darling; I don't blame you for any of this. I put the blame on your parents. It seems they did not teach you all the ins and outs of the Indian way of life, tradition, and culture. How are you supposed to know how it works and what your responsibilities are? I'm going to have a few words with your father," she continued stubbornly. "How could he not teach you about our way of life? It's so irresponsible."

"Responsibilities, what responsibilities?" he snarled. "Let me tell you about responsibilities, as I understand them. First of all, I am responsible for me, only me, and no one else. Somewhere down the line it's you, Mum and Dad, understand?"

It pained her to hear him say those words. She felt ashamed: "I said it before and I'll say it again, I don't know what they teach children in England, but I totally disagree with it. It's all about me, me, me, and there is nothing about *us*, nothing about what is best for the family." Jawali had been born into old traditions and believed in the old ways. Families, communities and respect for the elders were important to her. Her faith and nature were important for her, but she didn't see any of these qualities in her grandson. This saddened her enormously. The concept of an Eastern way of life made sense and had served her well throughout her life. She adamantly refused to alter her views to accommodate modern thinking, particularly her grandson's Western way.

"Secrets have a way of being found out eventually, don't they, Grandma?" Naj asked.

"It wasn't a secret as you put it, putter, it was all in the open. You met the girl and her family. You went through the ceremony. Everything took place above board and everybody was happy, including yourself. I really thought you liked the girl. She's lovely. She will easily fit into this family, no problem. She'd have made you a good wife and the two of you could have lived happily ever after."

"You tricked me, Grandmother, you tricked me. You made me look like a fool. All of you. How could you be so cruel to me? I'll never speak to Mum and Dad again, never," Naj said, looking at her angrily. "How could you do that to me? What have I done to you other than love you?"

An expression of pain fell across her face and she shifted uncomfortably. "Look, beta, we are all counting on you. You are the one who is going to take this family's name forward.

There is no one else; there's only you; if I had two or three grandsons it wouldn't be so bad. At least one of the others would have shouldered the responsibility in honoring the family's name and continuing its dynasty."

Temper turned Naj's eyes dark. He was completely baffled. "Are you crazy?" he asked her, wide-eyed and unable to believe what she had just said. "You are trying to emotionally blackmail me, aren't you? If you think I'm going to tolerate that, you are mistaken. It was a bad idea for me to come here in the first place. I don't know what I was thinking when I agreed to Mum and Dad's idea that I should visit you."

"Don't be hard on yourself, beta. Life is a journey full of challenges. You have to be strong to overcome them. Besides, you can't have it all your own way all the time. There are other people connected to your journey, important people, people who are close to you, people who care for you, people who are looking to hand you the reins of this family, this clan. You know who they are; your Mum and Dad and of course, little old me."

Naj listened silently, his head bowed. He was filled with anger and frustration, ready to explode. He was angry with her, his Mum and Dad, the girl's mother and the whole damn system. Most of all, he was angry with himself. *How could I let this happen to me, how could I? I'm supposed to be the smart one, for God's sake. I am a university graduate, educated. How could my own family do this to me? She's sitting there telling me that they did it for my own good. What kind of nonsense is that?*

Ramu knocked on the door and waited. He could sense all was not well with his masters. He knocked again. "Mata ji, it's me, Ramu."

"Yes, beta, come in," she commanded. The door opened just wide enough to admit Ramu, who slipped in and shut it behind him. Naj got up and walked out of the room. Jawali watched him leave. She felt sad and concerned. Suddenly the damage she had done dawned on her. The clock was striking. The air in the room was stuffy. She felt uneasy with herself. She went over to the window, pushed it wide open and looked out. The sky was grey. *What's going on today?* She thought. *The clouds, the sky, the sun, Naj, I have upset them all. No one is happy with me.* She pulled a small snuff box from her kamiz pocket. Snuff might raise her spirits. She had always turned to the little box of snuff, referring to it as her companion in time of need. She took a pinch and held her breath. Normally she would have sneezed several times but nothing happened, although she was ready to catch it in her handkerchief. Ramu watched from a distance until she had finished.

"Mata ji, shall I bring your afternoon tea in here or would you prefer to take it outside on the veranda?"

She shook her head and waved him out of the room with her hand. He left, closing the door behind him. Her mind was crowded with questions and worries: *It was foolish of me,* she thought. *The idea was not so good, it would have been kinder in the long run to tell him the truth about the arrangements. Had we told him, he would not have agreed to it; that is why we avoided telling him in the first place. We all hoped that eventually he would come round to the idea of marriage.*

Jawali went to bed early, without taking a shower or eating. She could not sleep that night. His words kept coming to her over and over again, as the clock struck every hour. She marched up and down in the room, going back to bed, lying down, sitting up, fidgeting, moving about, going to the window, looking at the clock, checking the time, pulling the curtains apart, then pulling them together. The dogs howled in the street. She felt hurt, and felt somehow like him. He was angry with her and she was angry with herself over the same issue. She must find a way to make amends. He was her own flesh and blood, her future, her dreams, her aspirations, her happiness, everything. *Rabbah, rabbah, teri he kirpa, tera he assra, I'm a mother, a grandmother, I feel torn and confused, I need your help in this hour of darkness. You have to show me the way.* Suddenly the words came to her: *Talk to him, heart to heart.* A change had come over her, the wisdom of elders, the softness of motherhood. *I have to talk to him,* she thought. *Explain everything, maybe he'll come around and see sense. It's no good for my blood pressure. I have to do something, it's not good for both of us; maybe it'll be easy to say I'm sorry and he'll forgive me with a look, a hug and a smile, that'll be nice, really, really nice.*

Jawali waited for the right moment, tried to talk to him, persuade him, time and time again but it seemed to make no impression on him. *Where is he this morning?* She wondered. *Has he gone for a run around the ground? Maybe he went to the market to clear his head or something.*

The next day was no different. A dark cloud hung over them both. He was horrified by her plot to get him married off. He felt that she had taken advantage of his ignorance and vulnerability and tricked him. He didn't go for a run or to the market. He was at the gurdawra then went to the masjid and to the temple next door seeking guidance, looking for answers. He didn't find any. Never in a milli-on years could he understand her actions, her plot. He could never forget all that. He thought she was calculating, cold and heartless. Later that evening the two of them were in the living room. As she tried to put her arms around him,

175

he pulled back. I can't. I don't feel like being hugged. Just… leave me alone, please." There were tears on her cheeks. She reached out once more to embrace him. He stepped back. Her lips trembled, and she was engulfed with frustration and pain. She felt failure.

"Why are you so mad with me?"

He glared at her and walked away without saying a word. His attitude and mannerisms became intolerable to her; he was like a dead soul. It mattered greatly to her. She resented his behavior. Her heart throbbed and her tiny body shivered with pain. She went into the bathroom and wept, her spirit broken. She could hear her cat crying with pain and knew that she had picked up her energies. At one point, Jawali was certain she was going insane. She was talking to herself and waving her hands in the air. Her eyes were watery and sunken, her vision blurred. She didn't know the answers. "Think woman, think," she muttered to herself. "You have acquired experience and now you must find the answers." She looked like a dried-up little woman. Nothing was coming to her, nothing at all. She scratched her head. *And what do I do now?* she asked herself. *He must have a heart of stone. He's a snob; he has to admit it. He has a heart of stone to push me away like that at my age. He has to be a heartless snob. Surely he ought to know better and show me some respect. Why is he so hard on me? Everyone makes mistakes now and then. He is stubborn like his granddad, stubborn as a mule.* Jawali thought of Naj constantly. She longed for his affection, his sweet words, his smile, his touch, his love, that was what she was longing for, that was all she wanted. Nothing more, nothing less. She felt alone. She had no one but God to turn to for answers. "Please God, help me to get through this," she said, looking up at the sky. "That is all I ask of you, that is all." She stood leaning forward, pausing for a moment. She had born her past struggles bravely. Now age was against her, her health degenerating. *Where are the answers to my prayers?* She thought. *Where is that calm ocean where only perfect winds blow?* She would have liked a granddaughter instead; another female in the family, that would have been nice, instead of this heartless brute. *She would have understood my feelings, my needs, love, duty, respect,* she murmured privately.

As the evening wore on, Jawali developed a nervous twitch just under her right eye. She was sure she was going blind. *It's all his doing,* she thought. Half of her couldn't be sure he hadn't deliberately done it just to be spiteful. But even if he had, he was still her child, her flesh and blood, her grandson, her family, her future.

CHAPTER NINE

It was Thursday morning and Naj was up very early. He had packed a few personal items into his rucksack and went to Kashmir without saying a word to his Grandmother. He left a message with Ramu about his planned return.

"He's gone," said Ramu. "He went after taking his breakfast early."

"Why didn't you tell me? Where do you think he's gone?"

"Kashmir, Mata ji."

"*Kashmir?*" her voice was sharp, ominous. Her face was anxious.

"Ji."

"No, he can't have. He would've told me so. He never said anything about going to Kashmir, not a word. Are you sure he said Kashmir?"

"Yes, Mata ji, Kashmir."

"No, I don't think so. I'll phone him. I ought to be able to track him down."

"He was in a strange mood, Mata ji, not his usual self. He said you shouldn't bother contacting him. He won't answer your phone."

Jawali looked at him, as the penny finally dropped. Her heart sank, and she was deathly pale. She knew Naj's stubbornness, it ran in the family, but she loved him deeply, and she would rather he had told her than left a message with Ramu. "Going off like that without saying anything to me!" she cried. She felt bitter and inadequate. "He was rather moody last night. I can't understand what's eating the boy. And why won't he answer my phone? Doesn't he realize I'm his family, his Grandmother, for God's sake? I'm worried sick about him. Is he so stupid?" *Naj did it on purpose just to get back at me,* she thought. *He deliberately planned it to hurt me. My own flesh and blood. What are they teaching children in England?* Jawali sighed in despair.

Naj failed to return and Jawali couldn't find any trace of him. He wouldn't answer her phone calls. She was frustrated, angry and sad. "Oh God!" Jawali's voice was laden with remorse. "What have I done? I've driven him away. He means everything to me." Jawali blinked, tears scalding her eyes. "Ramu," she ordered. "Find him for me and bring him back!"

Ramu's mouth tightened. He knew Kashmir was up in the mountain range. He had heard people talk about it, but didn't know where it was. He'd never been further than Hosharpur, an hour's bus ride away. Jawali knew the task was too great for little Ramu, but her options were limited. What could she do to bring Naj home? Ramu could see that she was upset, so he kept out of her way most of the time. He knew what she was like when she was in one of those moods.

The next morning Ramu came in bearing fresh fruit and flowers picked from the garden to cheer her up.

"Just leave them there," she said. He could tell she felt more lonely than ever. She was troubled and breathless, her heart pounding furiously. He wondered if she was going to die.

When Naj disappeared to Kashmir it was natural for Jawali to ask for a little chat with God. She was looking for divine intervention to watch over him and bring him back safe and sound.

On Wednesday morning, Jawali returned from the temple with prasad in her hand. "Ramu," she said, "here beta." He held out his hands and she gently placed a small dollop of prasad into them. "I guess I'll phone his Dad and let him know Naj has gone. He'll be concerned for him, of course. He knows Kashmir can be dangerous, especially if one is alone. I have done all I can. I have said my prayers for his safe return." There was nothing, not a sign of him, not a whisper from him. She waited, but he did not return, that day, that night, the next or the one after that. She phoned England, questioned, informed, shared, complained and protested. They had no knowledge of his whereabouts either. His cell phone was switched off. Frustrated and exhausted, she shut herself in her room, refusing to take food or water until the next morning. She went to the temple, alone, at dusk. Dressed in her husband's army shirt, salwar and the white shawl that covered her head, she prayed quietly for his safe return. In times of trouble she always went to the temple, to the masjid, to the church, to the gurdwara and other places of worship in the area. There were many. She believed in all of them equally. To her, they were where God lived; all of them were his homes. There was no discrimination in her soul, none whatsoever, not a thread. Her belief in God was her commitment, a duty, without reservation. Her affection for God was deep, her sanctuary in times of darkness and despair. Local children had reason to be grateful to her. She had always looked out for them, giving them sweets, taking an interest in them, and keeping them in check. They felt safe when she was around, because no one dared harm them in any way. She commanded respect from everyone.

Jawali returned home and went straight to the living room where Naj's photo hung on the wall. She stood and looked at it. Her lips formed the words. "I miss you". Tears glistened in her eyes.

Naj's visit to Kashmir was short. He returned after just four days. He had done a lot of soul-searching during his trip, and so had Jawali.

That afternoon Ramu was working in the garden, and Jawali was taking a seista on the patio with the mobile phone in her pocket. She was in considerable pain from not knowing where Naj was and prayed for him to make contact with her.

Ramu heard a car roaring up towards the house, and squealed to a halt in front of the wrought-iron gates.

Trilled at seeing Naj surge out from the taxi holding a small bag in his hand. Ramu delighted screamed the news at Jawali who almost had a heart attack with his high rate behavior of jumping up and down like a maniac and saying, "Mata ji, mata ji, it's Naj."

She was in a state of shock not knowing what he was saying and whatever's the matter with Ramu!

Naj tried hushing Ramu with a finger across his lips, for him not to say a word to his Grandmother, but he was too late. He plans to surprise his Grandmother were now defuncked.

"Oh, shut up," said Jawali. She succeeded at last in getting Ramu quiet. "Now, I got your intention do tell me what the problem is!"

"Mata ji look," said Ramu pointing his finger towards Naj

"Ah ha! The little rascal,"exclaimed Jawali, looking towards the gate pleased.

Ramu rushed to open the gates, Naj waddled in wearing a smile.

She forgave Naj for everything and was now full of sympathy for him. When he entered the patio, he planted a kiss on her cheek and gave her a big hug.

"Jianda rahai putter" (long shall you may live).

"I've missed you, Grandmother."

"I've missed you too, beta. Don't do that to me again. Going off without saying a word to me! I was worried sick. You could have been kidnapped, murdered or something. I remember reading an article in the Panjab Times only a month back about two foreigners being kidnapped by a group of bandits up in the mountains and they were demanding a large somes of cash for their release; when the ransom wasn't paid the bandits slit their throats and their bodies were found in the river. You should consider yourself very, very lucky my boy."

"I promise, I'll never leave this house again before telling you first."

"Good."

"Welcome back, sir." Ramu extended his hand.

"Mayherwanni, Ramu." They laughed.

"Your Hindi's getting better, sir."

"Thanks. I'm working on it."

"Ramu, go and make some tea for us," Jawali ordered.

"Yes, Mata ji."

"You must be really tired from your journey, putter. Come and sit down next to your Grandmother." It was a pleasant afternoon and they talked whilst taking their refreshment on the patio. "This home wasn't the same without you, Naj beta. These walls were crying out for you. Of course, little old me, I really didn't get a wink of sleep.

I kept looking out for you, thinking and hoping you were about to walk in through the gate any moment."

Naj sensed that his Grandmother had become increasingly attached to him. However, he was still angry. He was determined to speak his mind, but chose his words carefully: "I'm sorry my words had offended you, Grandmother, but it was wrong of you, very wrong. All of you deliberately plotted against me. I blame Mum and Dad more than I blame you." Jawali's frailty and time had softened things between them. She took a deep breath. She had decided to say nothing further on the issue. There was nothing to gain by playing games with the one she loved most. No more arguments. No more plots. No more engagements or arranged marriages. That was the way it was going to be from now on. She had learned her lesson. That evening they walked together in the garden and shared food from the same plate. She sat in her rocking chair, smiling with her wooden cane across her lap.

The next morning the air was moist and fresh but the sky was dirty grey and covered with fog. The sun gradually broke through and the fog lifted. The temperature rose steadily. Naj came out to the garden for a stroll, followed by his Grandmother. They walked around the vegetable patch admiring Ramu's creations and then sat on the patio.

"How was your trip, beta? Tell me everything," she ordered.

"Everything, Grandmother?"

"Yes, everything." She sat on the bench and he sat beside her, smiling affectionately and feeling guilty.

"It will take about a month, and I don't have that much time, I'm afraid."

"If that's the case, mere putter, then just the interesting bits."

Naj was just about to start when she interrupted: "Oh, I've never told you that I lived there for two years from 1935 when your granddad was transferred with his unit from Nakhlow to Kashmir just as we were getting ready for the Second World War. I remember it well, as if it was yesterday. It was so beautiful, especially in the spring. Of course, I was very young at the time and everything was an adventure for me."

"Yes, Grandmother, Kashmir is out of this world; the rivers, the rugged landscapes and the mountains, the people, the colors, the food and . . . everything, really. I wish I'd had more time."

"You could've stayed a few more days if you wanted to."

"I really wanted to but I had to come back for Vaisakhi. I couldn't afford to miss the Vaisakhi celebrations, could I?"

"If you had, beta, I would never have forgiven you."

"I'm not that silly, Grandmother. I wouldn't have missed it for the world."

"I should think so." She tilted her head. The cat climbed up on to her lap and she began stroking it.

"I also have to think about going back home to England. The return date on the tickets is only valid until next Tuesday so I'm on borrowed time."

The color drained from Jawali's face with the thought that her grandson was going to leave her so soon.

"Home? This is your home too, putter."

"I know, but England is where I belong. It's my birthplace and my home. All my friends are there. It's where my future is. You know, I'm really lucky; I've two homes, one in England and the other one in India. I know it will be hard for you when I'm gone, but I'm afraid I have to return." She wanted to hear him say that he'd be staying for a few more weeks. Amused for a moment by the absurdity of all of it, she laughed and then cried thinking about it. She had no idea when she'd see him again. All she could do now was to seize each precious moment and enjoy it.

Naj could see that the expression on her face had changed from one of happiness to sadness. He smoothly reverted back to Kashmir: "Grandmother, I wrote a piece of poetry on my Kashmir trip, just for you. Here it is."

Jawali was upset. Now there was nothing to say now. She wanted to say whatever came into her mind. But no, she couldn't afford to drive another wedge between them again. Life is short and precious. Her relationship with her grandson meant far too much. With that in mind, she straightened up, held her head and smiled at him.

"Ramu, where are you?" she called out. "Come and have a look, Naj has written a poem for me."

"There you go, Grandmother."

She held the paper in her hand and looked at it. She couldn't read, but she cleaned her spectacles just the same. "Damn!" she cried. "I wish my parents had sent me to school."

Ramu burst into the room with a grin on his face.

"Here, you read it for me, putter." The poetry was written in English but she wasn't to know. "Hurry up and read for me, you know I don't like waiting." She sat on the end of the sofa.

Ramu held the sheet in his hands. "It's in English, Mata ji, and I can't read English."

You and me both, she thought. "That's a shame. We have to do something about that, Ramu. You'll have to join an English class, beta, so that you can learn to read and write English."

Ramu looked puzzled. *I can't afford to pay for an English tutor on my salary*, he thought.

"I'll take care of the costs involved."

Ramu was so pleased. "God bless you Mata ji, thank you, thank you so much." *Once I have learned to read and write in English,* he thought, grinning, *I'll be able to read English newspapers and all the gossip in those glossy magazines and my girlfriend Sita will be very proud of me.* "Sir, you read it." Ramu handed the paper to Naj.

"Are you ready, Grandma?"

"Of course I'm ready, now start."

He looked at them both and began reading: *I have never been to Kashmir before in my life, but I have heard stories about it and had seen photographs of its rugged beauty in brochures, magazines, and films. Others tell me that the hills, mountains, valleys and rivers make it perfect for living like a Maharaja. In spring, the valleys are carpeted in beautiful colors with all kinds of flowers, crocuses and mustard flowers as well as fruit trees.*

Flat earth? No, not here. Visit Panjab if you want to walk on the flattest land in this part of the world. In Kashmir, the mountain ranges and the snake-like narrow roads will test one's courage and nerves.

One winter evening, as the sun was going down, I looked up with unblinking eyes and the sky suddenly turned red. The piece of earth I was occupying suddenly leaned towards the river. The earth stood still for a second and everything around me went very quiet. Then shaking and shuddering took over my senses; the skulls of curfew darkened my journey.

An earthquake hit the region. Thousands injured and dead. I grieved as the wind cried all night for my Kashmir and my people. With anger, I stamped deep on the earth's tectonic plates, but it was no use; the damage had already been done.

The sun stood for a moment at the end of the earth before it fell and darkness took over as the ghosts of the dead appeared all around me. I found myself asking questions: "Am I in the wrong place?" For some strange reason, I started to watch my own shadow, convinced that it was trying to tell me something.

A cold winter's wind shook the door and the remix song from the sixties classic film "Sangham" played in my head. Was it Mohammed Rafi or my mind playing tricks on me?'

Jawali looked though her glasses at Naj with enormous pride, feeling that somewhere along the line he'd stopped disliking his ancestral home, as had been his initial response. He'd come to appreciate and treasure it for what it was.

"It is wonderful, did you write this yourself?"

"Yes, Grandmother."

"For me?"

"Yes, Grandmother, just for you."

A grin as wide as the river Satluj appeared on her face. "You are a genius, do you know that? It is so real, so meaningful, I'm so happy. My grandson the poet! My own Bullay Shah and Ravindernath Tagore all in one." She looked into his eyes and smiled. "I'm so lucky to have you. Come here and let me give you a hug."

Jawali had always loved him; Naj knew that. Even during the fiasco about his engagement. He looked closely at her, thinking how gracefully she had aged. *Her way of life is so different,* he reminded himself. *I can't blame my Grandmother for behaving the way she did and wanting to see her grandson settled.*

Naj had brought Jawali a beautiful Kashmiri half-length jacket. He reached into his rucksack and pulled out the light-colored coat. "Try this on, Grandmother."

"What is it?"

"It's a Kashmiri coat."

She held it up, examining the color and design. "Thanks, how lovely." she said, taking his present. She was overjoyed. "I'll wear it when we go to Amritsar, on our trip to the Golden Temple."

Ramu whistled in the garden.

"Well put it on, I'm waiting."

"Oh, alright then. Give me a hand. Don't just stand there . . . It fits me just right."

"Do you like it?"

"Yes, it's really nice, it feels comfortable. Let me see myself in the mirror. Oh yes, I love it, thank you, thank you, thank you, beta. First you write me a poem and now this! I'm so pleased. Thank you, putter, you're so thoughtful." She reached over and gave him a big hug. Then she put her hands in the pockets and began to walk slowly through the door to the garden to show off her brand-new, beautiful Kashmiri coat.

"Ramu, Ramu, come and look, see what Naj has got for me. Isn't beautiful? Here; feel the material. It's soft like a baby's bottom, isn't?" she said proudly.

"Yes Mata ji, it is."

Jawali walked up and down the garden path with one hand in the pocket and the other holding onto the walking stick. She was tired. Later, she lay in bed awake with her eyes shut. The cat jumped on the bed and curled up beside her. She was almost asleep when Naj entered the room.

"What's the matter, Grandmother? Why are you lying down?"

"Oh nothing, I just felt out of breath for a moment, putter." She struggled to sit up, and the cat jumped onto her lap. He needn't worry about her, she was from the old world, made to last, she recovered quickly.

"I noticed that the sofa set had been moved against the wall. The room looks so large now. I like it, whose idea was it?"

"Mine of course, who do you think?" she replied.

"Keep it like that from now on, it's nice."

They sat and talked about life, heart to heart. It was as if nothing had happened between them. Their relationship was as solid as ever, as though a magnet inside both pulled them together.

The power of God is amazing, she thought. *It is his gift, his wish that the two of us are united again.*

The next day was the thirteenth of April, a very important day in the Indian calendar. A Vaisakhi day; the day for joy, happiness, and celebrations. A season of harvest festival, a day for giving thanks to God for providing good crops and the day when the tenth guru, Gobind Singh Ji, chose to formally establish the religion of Sikhism over three hundred years ago. Early that morning Naj, Jawali and Ramu dressed to pay their respects at their local temple, say their prayers and receive parsad. All over the Panjab the gurdwaras, temples, churches and masjids held special services in thanksgiving, followed by street parties and entertainments. Shopkeepers and the wealthy handed out free laddos and jaylaibees to the passing public. Everyone smiled, especially the street children who looked forward to this day of free food.

The Vaisakhi mela was about to go into action at the Dusshera grounds. The food outlets, the rides, bric-a-brac, clothes, live drama shows, the snake charmer and sports competition organizers were all hard at work, setting up, assembling, erecting and generally getting ready for the visiting public. Naj was excited at the prospect of playing a competitive game of football between his team, the

Khalsa College, and the army team. He had waited for this opportunity to test his fitness and impress his grandmother and the spectators with his trickery and skills. His spirits were high: *What could be more refreshing for a keen soccer player like me than a game of football?* He couldn't wait.

*

Naj and his Grandmother were both tired after the Vaisakhi festivities and the football competition. That evening they were sitting in the living room, watching an old Hindi movie on TV when the phone rang. Naj answered.

"Hello, who is it?"

"Never mind who it is. I want to speak with Jawali. Is she there? Tell her it's urgent."

"Hold on, I'll get her for you." He placed his hand over the phone. "Grandmother, it's for you," he said.

"Who is it?"

"The man wouldn't give me his name, but he asked for you and says it's urgent."

"Oh, tell him I'm asleep."

Naj looked at her in confusion "Don't you want to speak to him? He says it's urgent."

She made a face and shook her head. She knew who it was. She had been expecting a visit or a telephone call.

"My Grandmother is asleep right now. Can you call back in the morning?" He put the phone down.

"This guy sounded angry, Grandmother. Why didn't you speak to him?"

"Can't you see I'm tired? Besides, I didn't want to miss the juicy part of the film." Jawali hadn't been surprised when Moosa called. She had been expecting his call and was ready for him. Only yesterday, she had spoken to Sameena's mother to break off Sameena and Naj's engagement. Moosa's phone call made her little uneasy. *He's a nasty piece of work,* she told herself. *I don't wish to worry Naj over this, I'll have to think of a plan to keep him out of it; he has suffered enough already.*

The phone rang again.

"Don't answer it. It's him again, I know it." Her face paled. "He's not going to spoil my film. I'll phone him tomorrow."

They let the answering machine take over: "Hi, it's Mrs. Dulak's residence, if you wish to speak to Mrs. Jawali Dulak, please leave a message." The caller hung up. She knew it was him.

"That's his style," she murmured. Moosa knew exactly how to irritate people. He had a violent side to his character. He had already served a five year prison sentence for actual bodily harm and for attempted murder and had only been released recently. Everyone in his village thought he must have learned his lesson, but he was as mad as ever, always ready for a fight. His friends nicknamed him "Moosa the ready-steady-go man," and some called him "Moosa the short fuse".

Jawali kept expecting the phone to ring again. She wondered where he was calling from. Maybe from the liquor shop or the Dhabba food outlet. He could be phoning from around the corner or he could be anywhere on his mobile. *Maybe,* she thought, *he's out there behind the banana tree trying to mess up my mind.*

Half an hour later, the film had come to an end and Jawali retreated to her bedroom with a warm glass of milk. Naj had crashed out on the sofa. It was Ramu's day off. Outside, a storm was brewing. The banana trees swayed violently. Ramu had left his gardening tools outside. The wind tore small branches and twigs off the nimm tree. A banging, rattling noise from outside set Jawali's heart racing. She feared for herself and Naj's safety, thinking that there was someone outside trying to break in.

Maybe it's that madman Moosa, she thought. *You never know with him.*

Jawali got out of her bed in terror, grabbed her walking stick and walked across to the living room hoping to find her grandson sleeping on the sofa. He wasn't there. Panic-stricken, she called his name: "Naj, Naj beta, where are you? Answer me," Jawali shouted. She rushed across to his room and found him tucked away snoring under the comfort of the mosquito net, oblivious to everything that was happening outside. She felt relieved to see him lying there. She leaned over him.

"Naj, putter, are you awake?"

He raised his head from the pillow and looked up at her with one eye shut. "What's up?"

"I think there's someone outside."

"It's probably Ramu having a smoke."

"No, it can't be him. He's not here; it's his day off."

"It's probably nothing. Now go back to sleep, Grandmother. I'm tired."

"Naj, something is definitely out there beta, oothoe na [please come]."

"I bet you it's that darn cat of yours, up to no good."

"No, Shaanti's sleeping on my bed."

Naj sat up sharply. He could hear the noise coming from outside. He jumped out of the bed, pulled on his t-shirt and slipped his feet into his Jesus sandals.

"Give me your walking stick," he demanded.

"What are you going to do, beta?"

"You leave it to me. Just tell me where you keep your torch."

"I don't know. Ramu keeps it somewhere. Maybe it's in the cupboard in the kitchen, look in there."

Naj rushed to the kitchen with her stick in his hand and began to search the cupboards. Suddenly it came to him: "What do I need the flashlight for when we have a sensor light on the patio?" he muttered to himself.

As Naj opened the front door, a gust of wind pushed him back. His Grandmother, standing behind him, staggered back and fell to the floor. He pushed the door shut and knelt to support her. He feared the worst.

"Grandmother, are you OK?" Naj could see she was in a daze. He picked her up and carried her to her bed. He gave her a sip of water from a glass. She came around slowly and sat up, leaning against the headboard.

'Beta, I'm alright, don't worry," she said. "Just leave me here. Now go and see who's out there."

"Don't move from here until I get back," Naj said, pointing at her. His actions and mannerisms reminded her of her late husband. Holding his Grandmother's stick, Naj let himself out. The patio light illuminated the front of the house. He could see that the wind had torn away plants, flowers and bushes. Leaves and twigs were flying about in the gusts, and a sweeping brush was trapped against his Grandmother's bedroom window. It made a constant tapping noise in the gale force wind. A dog yelped. Naj stiffened a little, then quickly pulled the brush from the window and carried it into the house.

"Here's your burglar, Grandmother," he said sarcastically.

"What do you mean? That's a sweeping brush; even I can see that."

"It was this that was making the banging noise." He held out the brush.

"How was I supposed to know it was a brush making a racket? It sounded as though someone was trying to take the glass out of the frame. You think I'm going crazy don't you? Besides, it's always better to be safe than sorry." Suddenly, there was a flash of lightning. "I think the world is coming to end tonight. Just listen to all that noise out there. The gods are angry for some reason."

"Nothing is going to happen. Now go back to bed, Grandmother."

"You mark my words, putter. There's something brewing out there. I can feel it in my water." They went off to their rooms. *I'm not going crazy, am I?* She thought. *No, at least I don't think so, I'm sure there are people out there who think I'm completely mad. I do look like a crazy woman first thing in the morning, I really do, with my silvery thin hair sticking up all over the place. That creature Gollum in the Lord of the Rings film reminds me of myself sometimes. Maybe Gollum and I are related. After all, he has my jaw line and my nose and the name itself, Gollum. I'm sure it's an Eastern name. It has to be. The more I think about it, the more I'm convinced it's an old Indian name. I must admit, though, looking in the mirror I even frighten myself at times. I am definitely a frightening sight without my dentures. Ask my cat, she doesn't come near me until I'm wearing my dentures. Oh shut up, you stupid old fool, get some sleep.*

At dawn, morning prayers were broadcast, waking the neighborhood. Health-conscious individuals were out jogging, doing push-ups, stretching and Yoga. A lone cycle-rickshaw man waited for custom by the bus stop. At about five-thirty, a car pulled up outside 10 Dastoorba Nagar. Two men got out and casually walked through

Journey Home

the gates. Jawali was lying awake in her bed listening to prayers flooding through the window into her room, when suddenly she heard strange noises from the front of the house; something odd, something unusual that distracted her. She sat up, wondering what it could be. She listened. Who could it be at this hour?

"Ramu, is that you?" Jawali called out, forgetting he wasn't around this morning. He was at his parents' house, due back around seven, seven-thirty that morning. She waited for him to answer. "Where is that boy?" she murmured to herself, calling out his name once more. It went quiet for a few seconds. The sound of prayers mingled with that of birds singing in the garden. Her eyes were fixed to the door. There was nothing; not a sound from anyone. She reached for her walking stick from the side of the bed, then saw the door handle sliding downwards. The door opened and in came Moosa. He stood grinning.

"Who are you?" she said, raising her voice. "What do you want?" The grip on her stick tightened.

"Naj, Naj beta," she called, banging on the floorboards hard with the stick. A stranger in her domain, Moosa was a big man who frightened the life out of her. But, gathering her courage, she refused to show any fear. Fear was weakness, and she could not afford to show any form of weakness in this man's presence, this stranger with a grin. She concentrated her mind on her inner strength. She had plenty of that; she was not afraid of him. Jawali rose from the bed rather unsteadily, and moved forward to take a closer look at the stranger. She couldn't just sit there and ignore the man grinning at her.

"Namaste, massi ji," he said. The voice was familiar. She had heard it before, but failed to connect it with the man who stood in front of her. He had cold eyes and a tight, hard mouth. A cigarette dangled from the side of it "So you can speak after all!" she cried. "What's your name?" She moved towards him. Outside, nearby dogs barked as the milkman delivered the milk.

"Your eyesight is not so good these days, I hear. Let me help you. I'll switch on the light. Take a closer look; it's me, Moosa, your handsome nephew." He switched the light on and moved closer. "I'm sorry about this beard of mine. You see, they ran out of razors in the prison when it came to my turn." He rubbed his hand over his hairy chin. "That's a shame, you're not only blind, but crippled as well."

"Bacbass band karr (stop your rubbish), Moosa. It is the hour of God, a time for prayers. You should listen to the words of God sometime; it may help you change your ways. There are people out there humming his name this minute, whilst you are spitting out dirt. You're nothing but a goondah."

"You're not making much sense to me, massi ji, without those choppers. All you're spitting out is hot air," he laughed. She was not amused by his sick joke. What was more, she was not enjoying this encounter with Moosa, not enjoying it at all. She stood there, petrified and agitated at the same time. Oddly enough, she had quite forgotten what he looked like. She hadn't seen him for the last two-and-half years. All she knew was that he was in jail, serving time for cutting off another man's arm.

"I bet you can't believe seeing me here, massi ji?" he cried. "Me, your handsome bhateajah [nephew] Moosa under your roof, in your beautiful bungalow, having a civilized conversation with his kind hearted great massi ji." He lit another cigarette. She knew he had a screw loose. He was a man with mental problems. "How about a nice cup

Journey Home

of tea? I haven't had a nice cup of tea for ages. Tea with lots of milk and sugar. Three spoons, if I may."

"Tea? You'll get no tea here, you badmassh [rascal], the only thing you're going to get is this stick up your bottom!" she bellowed.

"Massi ji! I'm surprised at your language. What happened to all that wisdom and politeness?"

"Listen to me, Moosa, and listen well. I'm in a mood to forgive. Now is a good time for you to leave. If you do, I won't say anything to anybody. It's your choice."

"Ah, you think I'm scared of the police? What can they do to me?" he said, throwing his cigarette out the window. "See, I'm sensible, more sensible than you give me credit for. I could have thrown the cigarette on your bed."

Jawali had been standing on the same spot for too long. She felt weak. She needed to sit down, to take the weight off her aching feet and back. The color drained from her face. Moosa was her enemy. She hated him. She had half a mind to hit him over the head with her stick and send him on his way. He deserved it. But Moosa was the one in charge. He knew the layout of the house, he'd been here so many times in the past. When he was much younger, he and his mother had been regular visitors. He had been a nice, well-behaved boy in those days but his visits had become less and less frequent as he began to mix with older boys. Now, she knew, Moosa had other reasons for being here.

"Come with me to the sitting room. We need to discuss something very important," said Moosa, pointing to the door with a pistol in his hand. Seeing the pistol for the first time, Jawali felt a sick sensation in the pit of her stomach as Moosa moved closer.

"That's tough, really tough. Then again, it's easy to be tough when you're holding a pistol," she said, wiping the sweat off her forehead. Her fear abated. At last, she could bear it no longer. "Shoot me if you dare!" she cried out. "What are you waiting for?" Her voice was laden with fury.

"Don't worry yourself, old woman. I will if I have to." Moosa grinned, showing his rotting teeth.

Moosa's sidekick Rocky, a short man with a greased love-curl and bright dark eyes, forced Naj into the living room. Now he was joined by his Grandmother, and the two of them were made to sit together on the sofa. Jawali exchanged glances with Naj. In the street, a dog yelped as if someone had hit him with a stick or a stone.

Rocky was instructed to guard the door from outside, while Moosa strode up and down in the room, puffing at his cigarette. Naj and Jawali were petrified, not knowing what Moosa had in mind. She watched him like a hawk. *How dare he come into my house and turn us into his prisoners?* She thought. The two families had been related for generations, and Jawali had the respect and integrity of all their relatives and the local community.

"I had a funny feeling you were going to call round at some point. Tell me how much you need so that I can go back to sleep," said Jawali.

Moosa hissed: "If you think I've come for the money, old woman, then you're wrong. How dare you insult me twice in three days? First you insult my family's honor by cancelling Sameena's engagement with Naj, and now you're at it again. You're not thinking straight these days. One minute it's OK with you and the next minute you've changed your mind." The clock struck the hour.

Naj turned, darting a swift glance at his Grandmother. She looked pale, her lips compressed. He put his arm around her but then she turned to him and whispered "I'm alright".

Moosa began to move restlessly around the room, touching the items on display. He came to a round brass tray on the table. He inspected the item closely. "Uh-huh!" Moosa shouted. "I remember this thing, this belongs to my family." He held the tray to Jawali's face. "You stole this from my family!"

"Basaram, basaram, basram [shameless]!" she screamed at him.

"My sister gave it me on my sixtieth birthday." She attemp -ted to take it, but Moosa held it out of reach. "I'll take this with me, it belongs to my family."

People had told Jawali that Moosa had gone mad but she hadn't believed it until now. She heard him say something. Then he stopped and said something else. He accused her of things she knew nothing about. He roared with laughter without reason and the next minute went into a rage. Within seconds, he reverted to his goonddah-self. He wiped the tears from his face as he straightened up, then suddenly began to laugh again. There was a tap at the door. Could it be Ramu? Had he come early?

No; it was Rocky wanting a cigarette. Moosa opened the door and gave Rocky a lit cigarette. Then, closing the door, he turned to Naj. "So what do you think I'm here for?" Moosa asked harshly.

"I don't know; maybe you've come to clean our windows," said Naj sarcastically.

"That's a good one. I like that. 'Come to clean the windows', I take it, is an English joke. I'm not surprised, you being valaity and all that."

Naj turned to his Grandmother. "What's 'valaity'?" he asked.

"It's a Hindi word for someone from England," said Jawali.

Moosa laughed.

"So what it is you want from us?" she said bluntly.

"You know what I'm here for, but let me spell it out for you anyway. I want the wedding to take place; our families will be united, and everything will be hunky-dory."

"That's not going to happen and you know it, so why don't you just run along and leave us in peace?"

"You're not going to be difficult, are you? You see, massi ji, we've told everyone in the village and all our relatives about the rista between Naj and Sameena. Everyone is happily looking forward to the wedding." He took a deep draw from his cigarette. "Now listen, this is the deal. Naj, you are going to get all cleaned and dressed up, shaved and everything. At about eight-thirty we will all get in the car and drive to the City Marriage Registration Office. Sameena, her mother, and a few other relatives will be there waiting for us. At nine, we will be in the office and shortly after that you and Sameena will be legally married. How's that sound? Lovely jubbly, as they say in England."

"You can't be serious!" Naj complained.

"I'm always serious when it comes to my family's honor."

"You're not going to get away with this," said Naj.

Moosa grinned at him. They could tell he was serious.

"Just name your price, Moosa."

"We've been over this before, my dear massi ji. It's nothing to do with money. What we're talking about here is my family's honor, and no amount of money in the world can buy that. You of all people should understand that."

Jawali straightened up, her eyes focused on Moosa's face like a cobra ready to strike its prey: "I understand the need to uphold the value of honor and respect, but at the same time one needs to change with the times. These days, children are educated and they demand a greater choice in who they wish to marry. So you see, my Naj's happiness means much more to me than the honor you are talking about."

Moosa drew on his cigarette. He threw it on the floor and stubbed it out. "Yeah, yeah," he said. "It's all right; change the goal posts when it suits your own personal requirements."

Naj sat in silence, his arm round his Grandmother.

"If you had a child of your own, then you'd appreciate how important they are to their Mum and Dad. When God made you, he forgot to give you the brain."

"Shut up, old woman. Make the most of your yapping, cuz, you don't have much time left on this planet," Moosa said with a stupid grin.

Jawali's thoughts turned to Ramu. She wondered what had happened to him. *I hope he's alright,* she thought. There was no indication he had arrived. Maybe he had overslept or decided to take another day off. But wouldn't he have phoned or something?

Suddenly the door opened and Rocky stumbled in. He tried to speak, but words failed to come out of his mouth. "Ra-ra-ra," he mumbled, then fell and curled up on the floor with pain.

"God in heaven!" gasped Jawali, gripped with horror, her eyes fixed on Rocky. "Somebody help the boy!" she screamed.

"What's wrong?" Moosa asked.

"Take me to a doctor please, I'm in pain."

Suddenly, Ramu appeared. He was surprised to see Moosa, but wasn't sure what was going on. "What's wrong with him?" He pointed to Rocky.

"Go and get Doctor Persad, Ramu. Tell him to hurry." Jawali commanded.

Rocky screamed with pain. "Please God, help me!"

"It would be better to take him there, Ramu suggested. The bad boy Rocky's liver was messed up from years of alcohol abuse and cramps in his belly came without a warning. "Let's take him there,"said Moosa.

They put him in the car. Moosa at the wheel they headed for Doctor Persad's clinic. "This is not finished; I'll be back," Mossa yelled out of the car window.

Immediately, Jawali phoned the police and registered her complaint of harassment, intimidation and threatening behavior against Moosa. Later that day Moosa was picked up and taken back to jail for breaking the terms and conditions of his release.

CHAPTER TEN

It was hard for Jawali to accept that her grandson was going back to England. She did not want him to go so soon. Every time she looked at him, she had a sinking feeling in her stomach. It was so peaceful sitting in the warm garden. It was a moment to cling to and cherish; one she would remember when he'd gone, one she would take with her to her grave. "What's the rush, beta? Why do you have to go back so soon?" she asked sadly. "I would understand your rush to get back if you had a job to return to." She wanted him to stay until the monsoon rains, to experience it, to see it for himself how Mother Earth cleansed herself, to be part of the new awakening. And, of course, part of her wanted him to do what his heart needed.

"I would if I could, Grandma; it's my return ticket. Dad bought it on the cheap and there's no way to extend the date."

"That's your father's trade mark. He always looked for cheap deals, always. I don't understand him at all."

"Not to worry, Grandma. Now I know where you live. I'll be back again next year, and I promise to spend at leat three months with you next time."

Jawali sighed. "Next year, next year, that's what Darsh kept saying. 'I'll send Naj over next year'."

Twenty-four years had passed before that next year came, and then he only spent less than three weeks with me. Twenty days in fact. He spent four days in Kashmir. I waited a quarter of a century to be with my only grandchild and all I got was just three weeks. A crow flew by. She looked up at it numbly. I may not be here by next year for all he knows. She was restless. The thought of being alone again began to eat her up inside. Her chest tightened and her heart began to race. Deep down she knew that life might not give her another opportunity to spend time with him. She tried to put it out of her mind and went about her usual routine of visiting the temple, feeding the birds, inspecting the plants and flowers and chatting with her neighbors, behaving as if nothing concerned her. Naj went about his business, organizing his things, packing and repacking various items and putting presents, passport and flight tickets into his suitcase and rucksack. He took out the photos of himself with his Grandmother and held them to his face and smiled.

Things were packed and items organized. His passport and tickets had been checked and double checked. The weight of his luggage had been checked. Naj reminded himself of the twenty-five kilos maximum weight allowed by the airline. It was a beautiful April morning. Ramu had already loaded the suitcase and bag into the boot of the car and waited with the driver. Jawali put on a brave face, but inside her stomach twisted and turned. Taking a deep breath, she moved towards Naj. "You'd better hurry up," she said. "You don't want to miss your train, do you?"

Naj checked his watch again. "No, Grandma, that's not going to happen." *She should sit down,* she thought.

Ramu noticed Jawali struggling to stand upright, as her stick began to tremble.

Naj and Jawali walked slowly down the path towards the car. *I shall miss you,* said Jawali's smile. She embraced Naj and told him she loved him.

Journey Home

"I love you too, Grandma," Naj said softly. "Promise me you'll take care of yourself." He kissed her on the cheek one last time, and then sat on the rear seat of the car, whilst Ramu sat in the front along with the driver. Naj could see Jawali's small frame trembling as she stood by the gate, holding back her tears. She tried to put on a brave smile for him. The driver started the engine. Naj raised his hand, smiled, and said his farewell. Suddenly, Mrs. Datta appeared; she had been out shopping with a friend.

"Naj!" Mrs. Datta called, rushing towards them. "Beta, you're not going without saying good-bye, are you?"

"Yes, Mrs. Datta, I'm afraid so. I did call knock, but no one answered. I assumed both of you were out."

"Oh yes, I had to go with a friend down to the market." She looked over to Jawali, pale and distraught where she stood by the gate. "Don't worry about your Grandmother," she said reassuringly. "I'll keep an eye on her."

"Thank you, Mrs. Datta. I know you will. Please give my regards to Bonita.

Suddenly, the driver sneezed and Mrs. Datta's attention was distracted momentarily. She suggested Naj should wait a minute or two.

"Why?"

"Someone sneezed, beta. It's not a good sign."

"Not a good sign for what?"

"It's a well known thing, beta, when someone sneezes at a time of leaving, something unpleasant could happen on the journey. Therefore, it is wise to postpone it just for a few minutes."

Naj shook his head in amusement. He felt like saying 'screw you' but, chose to say nothing. He didn't wish to be rude in the presence of his Grandmother.

By now two minutes were up and Mrs. Datta smiled.

"Sir," Ramu said, "we have to get going or we'll be late."

"You have a safe journey back to England, and oh, say 'namaste' for me to your lovely Mum and Dad," said Mrs. Datta with a smile.

"Ok." He smiled back. It was a small mercy he had to make.

Naj looked at his Grandmother, who seemed so much older, and so frail. He felt sad, leaving her all alone. *She should move to England*, he thought, *where Mum and Dad could look after her, but she's so stubborn she doesn't want to leave her home, her friends, her community, her country, not at her age. She wants to spend her remaining days here, in the comfort of her home.* Jawali had been told England was too cold and alien for her and that she wouldn't be happy there, unable to communicate with the neighbors, the children and everyone.

Mrs. Datta moved close to Naj. "Here, beta; buy something on the way." She squeezed two hundred rupees into his hand.

Naj was surprised when he looked at the notes. *How generous,* he thought. *She's hardly family.* "Thank you, Auntie ji."

"You take care now," she whispered. Then she turned and stood by Jawali.

Suddenly, a car occupied by three people pulled up next to Naj's taxi. A man and woman stepped out of the car while the driver stayed put. The man was tall, about fifty something, with a flat North American accent. The woman was much shorter, with cropped jet black hair. She wore a traditional Panjabi suit. A relative, Jawali had known her in the past, but didn't recognize her now. Jawali remained cold but courteous until the pair explained the purpose

Journey Home

of their visit. They were, they explained, Sonia's parents. Both looked distraught and exhausted. The old lady was shocked and surprised, and Naj a little confused. There was a moment's silence. Feeling awfully weak, Jawali reached for her neighbor's hand.

"The power of fate was at work," she said. Mrs. Datta squeezed her hand and said nothing. "I think you'd better come in," she invited them.

Naj had had surprises before, but nothing like this. *Sonia and me, cousins? I don't believe it, it's so mysteriously unreal.* He looked at his watch to see what time it was. There wasn't much to spare. He had to get going. *What do I do now?* He asked himself. It was a most uncomfortable situation, and he felt torn. The timing was all wrong. They needed to speak with him, while he also had a lot of questions for them. He had a train to catch. A later train was not an option; he wouldn't make it in time for the flight. He saw the desperation on their faces and knew that he had to make a quick decision. Naj looked for a divine intervention. Then it came to him: "Why don't you both travel with me as far as Ludhiana? That should give us time to talk." There was no other solution, and this it made sense to everyone.

"Let's go, driver," Naj commanded, looking around for the last time. "I'll phone you as soon as I reach home, Grandma, OK, bye now," he said reassuringly as he wiped a tear from his cheek.

Jawali stood, her lips trembling. She was all alone once more. "Phone me when you get to the airport, putter." Mrs. Datta held her by the arm and comforted her as they raised their hands towards the departing car with tears streaming down their faces. Jawali said a small prayer, hoping he would reach home, safe and sound, and the two of them slowly walked back to the house. A few neighbors stood at their gates, watching them go. Tinku and Motto came running to wave goodbye.

When the car reached the main road, Naj looked through the back window. He saw his Grandmother grow smaller in the distance and a thin black dog standing watching from the nimm tree. *How strange*, he thought. They turned left, passed the Dusshera ground and after a few minutes they were out of the Cantt area, and over the bridge, along the dusty road and heading towards Jalandhar railway station.

"Stop by the shop," Ramu whispered in Mathew, the driver's, ear. They came to halt in front of a small hut backing on to a paddy field where a group of buffalo grazed in the early morning sun. A black crow took wing from a bull's back.

"Why are we stopping here?" said Naj.

"I'm out of cigarettes, sir; I need a cigarette."

"You know I need to catch my train and I don't want to miss it." Naj complained.

"Yes sir, I mean no, sir. I wouldn't let that happen, sir. This'll only take a minute, sir."

Naj checked his watch once more. He had thirty-five minutes before the train was due to leave for Delhi. "OK, you'd better hurry."

Ramu jumped out of the car and returned sharply with a packet of cigarettes and three bottles of Coke and they were off again. He smiled, handing Naj a bottle of Coke: "Here sir, take this."

"Thank you, Ramu. You are a real gentleman."

"I got you a straw as well, sir. I know you like to drink with a straw."

"What can I say? You are full of surprises, Ramu." Ramu lit a cigarette, feeling valued and proud. Then he leaned towards Naj. "When do you think you'll be coming back again, sir?"

"One day soon, I hope."

"Maybe next year, sir."

"We'll see, Ramu." Naj made a confident gesture with his hand.

"Did you enjoy your trip to India, sir?" Ramu asked politely.

"Yes, very much so."

Naj glanced out of the car. There were two pretty girls walking on the pavement.

"Would you like to take one of them with you to England, sir?" asked Ramu. Naj looked at Ramu and the driver. He felt oddly amused, but he had other things on his mind. *How strange,* he thought. *Sonia's parents turning up like that out of the blue.*

"In my view," said Ramu, "Panjabi girls are the most beautiful women in the world. They have everything, sir: soft, olive brown skin, long silky hair, beautiful features, culture and intelligence. Where else in the world would you find a woman with all these qualities, sir?"

Ramu's remarks gave Naj food for thought for a moment. "You may have a case, Ramu."

This pleased Ramu no end. His face lit up with the broadest smile Naj had ever seen. "Thank you, sir. I know I'm right. I have lived a little. I go to the cinema four times a week and have seen many films from all over the world. From what I've seen, there's no competition. Indian women are the best."

Naj smiled.

They were on a narrow stretch of road and the driver sounded horn at a rickshaw to make him move out of their way so they could pass. The man took no notice. Frustrated,

Ramu put his head out of the window and shouted: "Get out of the way, you idiot." The man kept peddling as fast as he could, looking over his shoulder at them. Eventually, after some distance, he gradually maneuvered out of their way, waving his fist in the air as they passed.

Naj shook his head. "It's madness," he said. "I couldn't drive on these roads myself. I'd probably get killed or kill somebody within five minutes." The others laughed. "Your famous drivers, Lewis Hamilton and Jenson Botton, they would be useless in India, sir. Even our ten-year-old rickshaw drivers would be too much for them to handle!"

Looking at a cycle-rickshaw and its young, skinny owner, Naj grinned. "Ah, yes. I think you might be right. Lewis or Jenson wouldn't be able to cope with Indian drivers coming at them from all directions. It's a crazy, crazy world, but I have to admit I love India regardless of all its problems. I'd like to come back very soon."

"It makes me very happy to hear that, sir," said Ramu. "Would you like Mathew to sing a tune for you in English?"

"You're having a laugh, aren't you?"

"No, sir. I wouldn't dream of something like that, no way; not me, sir. Seriously, sir, he's a good singer."

Naj looked at him. "Next you are going to tell me his friends and family calls him the Indian Elvis?"

"No sir, really, Mathew can sing. He's good."

"All right," he conceded. "Let's hear him. Go on then, Mathew. Make my day."

The driver cleared his throat and began to sing *Dangerous* by Naj's favorite band, U2. He knew the words by heart, although his accent and voice weren't like Bono's. Nevertheless, he did very well and surprised and amused Naj.

Journey Home

"He's good, isn't he sir? Maybe not as powerful as the Bono himself, but good nonetheless," said Ramu, grinning.

"You did alright, driver. You sure surprised me. You can't speak a word of English, but you sing well," he admitted. "Where did you learn to sing like that?"

"We Indians are very creative, sir. We can imitate anything given the chance," said Ramu with a grin. Naj couldn't help but smile.

At the station, Naj instructed Ramu to stay by the car and mind his things while he queued for a ticket. The station was packed with people, some squatting, some lying on the floor and others pushing and shoving for travel permits. Naj tried to spot Sonia's parents, but it was impossible. The train arrived at the station some twenty minutes early, surprising everyone. It was unusual for an Indian train to be early. Usually, they arrived late. Naj bought the ticket and, with Ramu carrying his luggage, elbowed past passengers onto the train in time to find a seat in the overcrowded carriage. Naj wanted a seat by the window so as to see a bit more of the scenery, but it wasn't possible. *Hey this is India, after all,* he reminded himself. *I'm lucky to get a seat at all.* He looked out for the Canadian couple for the last time, but they were not there. *Ah well,* he thought, *maybe they'll contact me in England.*

Ramu stood on the platform by Naj's carriage, almost in tears. Suddenly, he ran back to the station, returning a few minutes later with a magazine and some pakurras.

"Sir, these are for you, please take them. It's something for the journey. Goodbye."

Naj was just settling into his seat when Sonia's parents suddenly turned up with the ticket inspector. They had managed to bribe him for seats next to Naj. Sonia, it turned out, had been Naj's distant cousin, from his mother's side of the family. Her real father had died in Canada when she was a baby, and her mother had come to India and remarried a man named Ajit, returning to Canada two weeks after their wedding. They had not stayed in touch with their immediate families or returned to India until now. Sonia's mother turned out to be a charming woman. In fact, they were both nice. Oddly, they reminded him of Stephen and Sally Holloway, his neighbor, to the left. Naj also discovered that Sonia had had no idea that Ajit was her step-father. This had been kept secret from her. Naj found this odd and disturbing. It seemed pointless to question them about it. They must have had their reasons. Besides, what right did Naj have over them? He had only known Sonia briefly. He wondered if Sonia knew the truth about her father. There were many questions, but very little time. They exchanged contact numbers and agreed that they would call and arrange to meet up in England when they were on their way back to Canada.

An hour later, everyone had settled down and Naj found enough space to straighten his legs. Thoughts about his experiences in India began to flood his mind. He had come to his ancestral home by chance, because of a devious ploy of his family, his elders. England was his home, but Naj could no longer discard or turn away from what had happened. This trip, this extraordinary journey, had been special and a real eye opener. He knew that something had happened, changing him forever. India had been an adventure like an undiscovered valley, a garden, a river full of surprises that had, at times, taken his breath away, especially the trip to Kashmir. Everything came together: the turns, corners, highs, lows, scenery, colors, rising and setting of the sun, the midnight moon, the stars, the hassle, the

Journey Home

bustle, the tussles, the smell, the animals, birds, bees, trees, fields, temples, mosques, landscapes, rivers, and mountains. It had never occurred to him that he would fall in love with India in such a short space of time. The effect of everything in his life was immeasurable. There was no mystery as to why. The first few days had been very painful. He had lost someone very special without warning. Travelling had given him a new outlook on life, changing everything for him, and altering his perspectives on lots of things. He was not the same person he had been three and half weeks ago. He had altered for the better.

Naj thought about Lucy. She was a tender, beautiful girl and he loved her with all his heart. He knew that his journey had impacted on his mind, his life. Now he questioned things that had never bothered him before. It was impossible not think about the challenges he would have to face. They would have to face them together. They would bring up mixed-race children; Lucy had her own faith and beliefs. How would that work for their child, for him, for her? It had all seemed very clear before the trip, but now he started to feel the pressure of two cultures and faith systems. What would he do now? He felt confused and had no idea where it was going to go. Could he let life take its course and hope for the best?

A ticket inspector walked into his carriage, disturbing Naj's thoughts.

Naj was half way to Delhi when John Lennon's "Imagine" began to play on his cell phone, waking him.

"Hello, who is it?"

"It's me, Tom."

"What's up, brov?"

"I thought I'd just give you a ring to see how you were doing."

213

"I'm fine, but you sound nothing like your usual self. What's up?"

"You don't want to know."

"It sounds serious, man. Come on, try me; we're mates, aren't we?" Naj suspected something was wrong from the tone of his voice.

"Well, you're going to tell me. I told you so." Tom let out a long breath and groaned, as if he was in pain.

"Now you've started to worry me. Hurry up and spit it out. It's that woman's husband, right?"

"Uh."

"I knew it. I told you, you fucking idiot, you were going to get caught out. You never learn, do you, dumb bastard? Where are you now?"

"You aren't going to believe this, but I'm in hospital."

Naj pictured Tom in hospital all bandaged up with tubes connected to his body. He lost his cool. The man sitting next to him gave him a stare.

"You idiot, I kept telling you that woman's bad news, but no, you thought she smelled of roses every time she farted. Didn't I tell you enough times that bloke was going to put you in your grave if he ever found out? You just laughed it off, like you always do. God, you make me sick."

There was silence for a few seconds. A young woman seated across the aisle whispered something to an older woman next to her. The older woman glared at Naj with a face that said, "Mind your language, young man." He looked at her but didn't see her.

"Not as sick as I feel right now, believe me. You wouldn't want to be in my shoes right now," said Tom.

"I take it you've still got arms and legs attached to your body."

"Just about. They are still here but the doctors had to do a reconstruction job on me. The fucking bloke broke my nose, my right arm and two ribs. There were cuts and bruises to every part of my body. The nutter tried to finish me off for good, but the doctors managed to save my life." A nurse came and told Tom to keep his voice down. "Sorry, love."

"What was that? I didn't hear you properly," Naj said.

"It was nothing, bruv. Anyhow, I've been here for a week and you'd have trouble recognizing me if you came in to see me today."

"Shit man, you're so fucking stupid. What's happened to the fat cow's old man?"

"My old lady says he was picked up by the law, and is banged up at Pentonville in London. She told me he's been refused bail. The police came in the other day and took my statement. They told me that they couldn't do anything until they had spoken to me."

"It's a relief to hear he's locked up. Now listen, I'm on my way back and should be with you in less than twenty-four hours. I'll drop by with a bunch of grapes."

"Thanks, mate. You have cheered me up no end. Don't bother with grapes or anything. I'm having difficulties chewing my food."

"Idiot the grapes aren't for you, you tosser! I'm bringing them for me."

"Don't make me laugh, it hurts," Tom groaned.

"OK, see you in a day or two. Just hang in there, bruv."

"Bye."

After he hung up, Naj's focus shifted from enjoying the Indian countryside to feeling sad about his friend. *The man is a complete idiot, a total asshole, but I have to admit I love him to bits. He's been part of my life since we were kids, and I know he had a rough time growing up. We all make mistakes and often learn from them, but not him. He seems to like the replays for some reason. Maybe for the thrills and excitement. He needs to grow up before it's too late. Maybe this experience will help him to exercise his brain a little.*

*

Right on schedule, Naj's plane landed at Heathrow. For Lucy, the last three or four days had seemed endless. Night times were the worst. She had been unable to sleep. She watched the activity at Arrivals, seeing people greeting each other, smiling, hugging and kissing. She checked the monitor. Naj's baggage was in the hall. *He will be here any moment now,* she thought. Her heart raced with excitement and her eyes glowed in anticipation. She wanted to stand still like the other people waiting by the barriers, calm and composed. She wanted to stay quiet and be patient, but she couldn't; it was too hard for her. She wandered over to the monitor again, just to satisfy herself once more. Then she leaned on the barrier, much closer to the exit doors. She wore a brand-new three-quarter-length red coat. It was cold, she wanted to dress to please, and it was her twenty-fifth birthday. She wondered if Naj remembered. If not, she had decided not to say anything to him until they reached home. With eyes burning for a sight of him, Lucy raised herself on her toes to see him amongst the arriving passengers. *Where is he, what's delaying him?* She wondered. She glanced in the direction of arrivals, and then saw a security woman looking at her, stopping her dead in her tracks. There was nothing she could do but wait patiently like everyone else for what seemed like an eternity. *I hate waiting*, she thought.

Journey Home

Lucy checked her watch once more. She had been waiting for more than forty minutes, her anticipation turning into frustration. She was no longer sure when she would see him. She was almost tearful. *I hope he hasn't missed his flight; I hope he is all right and nothing's happened to him.* She tried phoning him on his mobile, but each time she was greeted by the voicemail. With so many people milling around, it was hot and she very nearly burst into tears when she saw Naj coming towards her; tall, tanned, and handsome, the love of her life. He was pushing a trolley loaded with a large suitcase and with a bag on his shoulder. He spotted her instantly, smiled and waved to her. She screamed with delight and waved back at him.

"He's here!" she said, raising her hand victoriously as tears ran down her face. Naj was wearing a brown t-shirt with *I love India* printed across the front. *My Naj, he's so* sexy, she thought.

A number of planes had landed within minutes of each other and with them came hundreds of passengers pushing luggage-filled trolleys, carrying things in their hands and bags on their shoulders, eyes searching for their waiting loved ones. Amongst them several taxi drivers waited, holding placards with their passengers names. Lucy elbowed her way through the waiting crowd and ran to Naj. She flew into his arms and he held her in a bear hug. They kissed as others pushed past them.

"I've missed you," she said.

"It's good to be back."

"Let me carry your bag."

"Thanks." Naj lifted the bag and passed it to her. Their eyes met and the intensity of his stare held her motionless. "You look different," Naj whispered into her ear.

"Oh, you've noticed," Lucy murmured back. "You like it?" she said, her hand brushing her hair. "I had it done specially for you." She smiled at him.

"It's nice," he said. "It suits you."

Lucy was pleased that Naj approved of her new darker hair. Eager to get home, Naj pushed his trolley towards the exit, nearly colliding with another passenger, who appeared to be hot under the collar. His breath smelled of drink as he came close.

"Why don't you watch where you're going?" the man cried. Naj apologized. "You will be sorry if you don't watch it." the man continued.

"I've said sorry. What more do you want?" Naj protested.

Lucy's face reddened with anger. "What's your problem?" she said to the man, who towered over her. He turned to Lucy as he struggled to maintain his composure. "Look, lady," he began, but before he could mutter another word a friend grabbed his arm and dragged him away. The crowd looked on as a security man arrived.

"Sorry; he's had a little too much to drink, he doesn't know what he's saying," the man's friend apologized.

Lucy looked at Naj. "Welcome home, darling." They laughed. Although it was middle of April, Naj felt the chill.

"You better put something on or you'll catch a cold, darling," she told him.

"You're right, it's much colder than I expected. Pass me that bag for a minute, please." Naj took out a thick jumper and slipped it on. "It was thirty-seven degrees in Delhi when we took off," he said as they walked towards the exit. The smell of fresh roasted coffee greeted them and they stopped. Naj looked at Lucy. "You know what?"

"What?"

"I fancy a hot cup of coffee."

"You do? OK, it's my treat. You go and take a seat over there and I'll get the drinks," she said, pointing to a seating area.

They sat at the table and Naj took a sip. "This taste amazing and the smell . . . The coffee in India tasted nothing like this. That was the one thing I missed most."

"Just the coffee?" Lucy was disappointed by Naj's list of the things he missed most, and that he chose coffee over her. She waited for his apology. He looked, noticing the change on her face, and then it came to him: "Oh, oh, I'm sorry. I didn't mean it that way, darling. Of course I've missed you the most, what are you talking about?" He planted a kiss on her cheek. "I was just talking about things, you know what I mean. I'm sorry; I wasn't thinking straight. You can see I'm tired, the immigration idiots gave me grief for nothing. They probably thought, 'Ah, another young Asian male returning from India or Pakistan, he's got be linked to a terrorist organization or something', and that drunk made it even worse."

"What happened at immigration?"

"I'll tell you all about it when we'll get home," said Naj. It was too soon to tell her everything that had happened.

"So that's why you were late coming out."

He nodded.

"I'm sorry darling, I'm so sorry," she said softly, clinging to Naj's hand.

"Let's finish this and go home." Naj gazed at her. "The first thing I need to do is take a shower and then a change of clothes."

"I *thought* you smelled a bit funny," said Lucy, teasing him.

"Oh-ay, that was uncalled for!" He poked her.

219

"I was just kidding," she murmured, cuddling him.

Naj and Lucy finished their drinks. With their arms around each other they headed towards the Piccadilly Line Tube Station.